ALBANY

PART THREE

What Happened in Costa Rica

Nigel Heath

This is a work of fiction. Names, characters, business, events and incidents are the products of the author's imagination. Any resemblance to actual persons, living or dead, or actual events is purely coincidental.

Copyright © Nigel Heath 2022
This book is sold subject to the condition that it shall not, by way of trade or otherwise, be lent, resold, hired out, or otherwise circulated without the publisher's prior consent in any form of binding or cover other than that in which it is published and without a similar condition including this condition being imposed on the subsequent publisher.
The moral right of Nigel Heath has been asserted.

ISBN 9798362134730

My grateful thanks in the preparation of Albany House are due to Marc Bessant Design, my wife, Jenny Davis, Mary Watts and Alexandra Bridger for literary support, to artist Maureen Langford for the cover picture and to my walking companion and poet, Peter Gibbs, for his technical support. Peter's poetry anthology, Let The Good Rhymes Roll, is also published on Amazon.

Chapter 1

The three Canadian tourists in their top of the range hire car, caught the rousing sound of a brass band as they drove along the shade and sunlit lane a few moments before emerging into the small picturesque North Devon village of Little Oreford.

They continued slowly along beside the green, admiring the row of chocolate box thatched cottages on the far side, before pulling up outside The Oreford Inn.

The music appeared to be coming from behind a large house beyond and at right angles to the hostelry and Jonathan Meyer casually remarked on this while checking in to the coaching inn for ten nights with his parents.

"Oh yes sir. It's a birthday party being celebrated by the family at Albany House and I'll be popping over as soon as I've booked you in," explained Annie Smart, the duty manager, noticing that this reservation had been made in a call from Toronto several months earlier. He was, she thought, quite an attractive man of about the same age as Corinne Potter, the still single hotel manager, and if she wasn't happily married to Bob, who ran a chauffeur-driven limousine business, she'd quite fancy him herself. It was an anathema to Annie that Corinne had yet to find a partner because she knew there had been several affairs that had never quite worked out.

"And what brings you to Little Oreford, Mr Meyer?" might I ask, she enquired. "My forebears emigrated to Canada from these parts early in the nineteenth century and I'm accompanying my parents on a discover our roots tour," he explained.

Oh, so he might be single, Annie thought, spotting that he wasn't wearing a wedding ring, but quickly forgetting the conversation as she handed over to a colleague and hurried up the drive to the big house to join Bob, who was already at the party.

Thoughts of their personable guest floated back to her later while family and close friends were sitting around a long party table on the raised patio overlooking the rear garden. The band had long since packed up and gone, as had all the village guests, and everyone remaining had consumed more than their normal intake of chilled white wine and were in a contented and contemplative mood as they relaxed in front of the party debris.

"Our new guests are Canadians called Meyer on a discover their roots tour and arrived later than expected, which was why I was delayed coming over to your party Charlie," Annie explained. She was blissfully unaware of the silent shock wave, her so seemingly innocent remark had just created. For Charlie Andrews, nee Potter, whose 75th birthday they'd all gathered to celebrate, the name 'Meyer' was one of enormous significance.

She'd definitely had more to drink than normal, not that she ever needed alcohol to help her hold forth and be the life and soul of every party, but hearing the name 'Meyer' sobered her up in an instant. How could it not when it was one Brad Meyer from Toronto on a flying visit business trip to Bristol, who'd left her pregnant with her twins Corinne and Laura after a one-night stand in the city's smart Star Hotel, a lifetime ago.

He'd left her all his contact details before they'd parted, promising to send her an airline ticket just as soon as he got home, which of course, he never did and she'd never heard from him again.

"A penny for your thoughts, Ma," broke in her wealthy property developer stepson, James, who'd flown in from his home in the Caribbean to celebrate Charlie's birthday. He'd learned the quaint English saying as the seven-year-old son of widower and now the late Hugo Andrews, whom she'd met and married while working in the hotel industry out there.

"It's all right, Jimmy," for that's what she'd always affectionately called him. "Just a passing shadow."

On either side of her at the table were Corinne, who ran the Oreford Inn, and Laura with her husband Ben Jameson, who lived at Albany House and ran the award-winning Old Mill House Visitors' Centre and Craft Workshops at the other end of the green. Next to them was their son, and Charlie's grandson Luke, a climate change scientific researcher, who'd recently returned from spending six months at The British Antarctic Survey base. He'd arrived home full of disturbing facts and figures about how the world was now warming up so rapidly that unless all the major nations stopped burning fossil fuels asap, which of course, it was highly unlikely that they ever would, then the planet could pass the point of no return in his life time.

Laura had taken him aside earlier and asked him not to go on about climate change at the party for fear of casting gloom over the happy occasion to which he'd responded with a typical rolling of his eyes.

"Mum, as if I would," but she knew better.

Their younger daughter Lottie and husband Andy Taylor, The Oreford Inn's chef, had left the happy family gathering to take their exhausted, five-year-old twins Jack and Hannah, home to their apartment at nearby Little Oreford Court, Charlie's mini stately home for the past five years. Annie and Bob also lived there in the stable annex and would be taking Charlie home later in Bob's beloved classic Bentley.

Sitting at the far end of the table were her childhood friends, brother and sister Robin and Margo Lloyd, who'd lived in the small picturesque village for many years and were the wealthy owners of Albany House, The Oreford Inn and of the Old Mill House Visitor's Centre and Craft Workshops, all leased to the Jameson family at peppercorn rents.

All three life-long friends were still in robust health, despite their steadily advancing years, which was why they'd not given any serious thought to what provisions they should make for the future. It was Charlie, always the leader in their wildly free childhood days roaming the fields and woods around Little Oreford, who'd eventually raised the question.

It was over supper the previous evening, at her period home, which she'd purchased outright, soaking up just a little of the interest in her inheritance fund, administered on her behalf by her stepson.

"I have a plan," she announced to Robin and Margo after they'd finished their first course. "Oh no not another one!" said Robin, looking across at Margo, as all three shared the joke, which had endured since childhood. "Is it perhaps time that we should think about what happens here after we've gone?" she asked quietly. "That's easily answered," replied Robin.

"We've left everything to Laura and Corinne, to include separate lump sums for Luke and Lottie and we'd rather thought you'd be doing more or less the same Charlie," he told her. "Yes, that is what I am going to do, but in the meantime, I wondered whether we might also set up a Jameson Family Trust Fund and each contribute a sizable sum so that we can see our young people taking advantage of it now to further the family business enterprises, rather than waiting until after we're gone. I've spoken to Jimmy about it and he says there would be no problem and, depending on how much we threw into the pot, it would reduce the amount Laura Ben and Corinne would have to pay in death duties when we are all gone," she pointed out.

"Well Charlie, that is something to think about," said Margo, looking at Robin. His thoughts had flown straight to his model village, which had taken on a new lease of life in a corner of their large cottage garden following the arrival of Lottie and Andy's twins.

He'd created it some thirty years earlier after he and Margo had taken early retirement from their respective careers, sold their 1960s acquired London homes for a small fortune and retired to their parents' cottage beside the green.

So perhaps a trust fund would allow the family to acquire, renovate and rent out several properties that, for one reason or another, had become run down, he reasoned. There was, for example, the former Oreford Hunt kennels, a dilapidated Victorian red-brick building, now completely overgrown and literally falling down in woodland close to the village allotments.

Robin had long since realised why he'd spent so many hours creating and working on his now much revived model village.

That was because in his younger Civil Service days, he'd become heavily involved with the creation of one of the country's post-war new towns. It was, he realised, some deep-seated desire to create order, a bit like that handful of enlightened and philanthropic Industrial Revolution factory owners who'd created whole new mini towns, like Port Sunlight, for their workers and their families to live in decent conditions.

"Come back to us, Robin," said Margo, seeing that her brother had suddenly slipped off into one of his 'daydreams,' as she called them, which had become worryingly more frequent of late.

"I think a trust fund is a sound and sensible," he said.

"And I agree with Charlie that it would be great to see the young people taking advantage of it now while we're all still alive and kicking, So why don't we each contribute £500,000, giving them £1.5 million to be getting on with while also including a top up provision," he suggested.

"I really think you must be psychic, Charlie," he continued.

"It was only a couple of weeks ago that I had a heart-to-heart with Ben, who is feeling in need of a new direction," he told them.

"For years, we all know he had a big project and that was raising enough cash to get the old mill working again, and eventually succeeded in doing so. Margo and I offered to help several times, but he always refused saying we'd been more than generous to the Jameson family already and that by adding value to the mill, he'd be paying us back, seeing that it belonged to us anyway. But now he's feeling a bit at a loose end and in need of a new challenge.

It's all right for Laura because she has the running of Albany House and helping with the twins to keep her fully occupied and she's quite territorial over her responsibilities," he pointed out.

It didn't come as any surprise to Margo or Charlie that Ben had confided in Robin because the two had become very close over the years with Robin regarding Ben as the son he'd never had.

"So what do you think Ben and the girls would want to do with this £1.5 million if we did set up a separate Little Oreford Development Fund with us acting as trustees, brother?" Margo asked. "That would be for them to decide and for us to agree," he replied.

"So, a new trust fund it is then and I will now talk to Jimmy about how we proceed from here," said Charlie.

Chapter 2

The unexpected tapping of a dessert spoon on a wine glass, caused a silence to descend over the happy family gathering. Charlie had waited until her granddaughter Lottie's husband Andy had returned to the table having left their twins with Heidi, their regular Saturday child minder, before speaking.

"As Margo, Robin and I are not getting and younger and here we all are celebrating my 75th birthday, we have a special announcement to make. She paused. "Well, it's not so much an announcement, but more a proposal for you all to consider as one happy and very united family," she said looking slowly around at them all in turn. Everyone wondered just what was coming next. "Firstly, Annie and Bob, I want you to know that after all your great kindnesses to me, over the past years, here and when I lived at the Ocean View retirement hotel in Sidmouth, I regard you both very much as members of our extended family." There was a spontaneous ripple of applause around the table. Everyone appreciated just how much Annie and Bob had done to support Charlie and the whole family after she'd acquired Little Oreford Court and they'd come to live in the apartment above the old stables.

This was especially true for Lottie and Andy, who'd moved into the adjoining annex immediately after their village wedding, and relied a lot on the couple before and after their twins were born.

Both could not help remembering the dramatic night that Lottie's waters had broken unexpectedly and their dash to the County Maternity Hospital in the back of Bob's Bentley.

"Robin, would you like to take over now?" asked Charlie as all heads turned towards him. "It's quite straight forward really, in that after Charlie has made bequeaths to you Annie, to share with Bob, all her assets, together with ours on our deaths, will go to you Laura, Ben and Corinne with separate sums for you, Luke and Lottie, to help you along life's highway." He paused, looking around at them all. "However, rather than waiting until we are gone, we thought it might now be a good idea to set up a Jameson Family Trust Fund with a capital of £1.5 million to be managed jointly by you all and to be used to further expand the family business in any way you all see fit. Initially, Charlie, Margo and I will act as trustees and have the final say over the release of funds."

A few seconds silence settled over the table as the younger Jameson's absorbed this exciting proposal, and then an elated Ben was the first to respond. "It sounds an amazing proposal to me, but what do you think Laura and Corinne?" he asked.

"Dear Mum, Robin and Margo, you've already been so generous to us all, but if you're sure you want to do this, then yes please," said Corinne, and Laura agreed.

"If I might also say a few words now," broke in Jimmy. "It really is a great pleasure for me to be part of such a close and united family and I know it will give Ma, Robin and Margo even more pleasure to see you all benefitting from part of your inheritance now rather than later."

But Charlie was only half listening to her stepson because her thoughts were still being dominated by Annie's casual news that a Canadian family called Meyer had turned up and checked in to the Oreford Inn on her birthday afternoon.

Luckily, neither Corinne nor Laura had picked up on the conversation, or they too would probably have grasped its enormous significance. So, what should she do about it? That was the question, but then the answer came to her and it was obvious really. She would take Corinne aside later and ask her to see what she could find out about these Canadians, who had suddenly arrived in their midst. It was at that moment that Robin stood up, albeit slowly as he was as near to being inebriated as he had been for many a year, and a glass was tapped for silence for a second time.

"Dearest friends as Margo and I are beginning to flag after a most joyous and memorable afternoon and evening of celebrations, I think it's time we took our leave, but before doing so, I would like to raise a finale toast to Charlie, our oldest and dearest friend," he announced. "To Charlie," everyone repeated after with a scraping of chairs, they'd all got to their feet and joined him in a standing ovation.

Charlie sat there for a few moments in the expectant silence that followed, looking around at her beloved family. "There are no words that would do justice to how I feel about you all so I'm simply going to say thank you. Thank you everyone."

Another spontaneous round of applause erupted, signalling the ends of the celebrations. It was now that Charlie called Corinne aside. "I know everyone will want to stay and help Laura and Ben clear up, so might we go back to the residents' lounge because there's something I want to discuss with you dear?" Corinne also felt she should stay and help, but on the other hand, they were having a busy evening at the inn, so she really did need to go back and keep an eye on things.

Luckily, the small residents' lounge was unoccupied so Corinne left her mother settled in a comfortable leather arm chair while she went on a quick tour of the busy kitchen, restaurant and main bar area to make sure that all was running smoothly.

"Now what is it you want to talk about Mum?" she asked, after returning with a large mug of strong black coffee to satisfy her craving.

A few minutes later, a mutual silence descended as Corinne internalised her mother's surprising news that a Canadian family from Toronto with the same name as her father, were now settled under their roof, "I know that Meyer is not really an uncommon surname, but just how many can there be in Toronto who are not in some way related to one another?" she wondered.

Charlie reached over and took her hand. "I have this strong feeling that these Meyers just might be related to your father, and it's left me finally wanting to know what actually became of him," said Charlie quietly. "And not only that, I have this strange feeling that something else is going on here, something that is somehow tantalisingly beyond our grasp or understanding."

Corinne nodded in agreement. It just had to be something more than the most amazing coincidence, that she and her sister Laura had found their way back to Albany House and that now these Canadians with her father's name had actually turned up at the inn on the very day of their mother's birthday. It somehow defied understanding.

"Mum, it's often said there's more going on in heaven and earth than we shall ever know and these coincidences must be a classic example," she said quietly.

"So look, I will do what I can to glean some more information from the Meyers, and, if by some amazing chance it turns out there is some connection, I will do my best to find out what happened to my father, even if means flying out there," she promised. "Would you dear?" said Charlie. "Yes, I would Mum because, to tell you the truth, having a father you've never known, does leave a hole in one's life and a sadness that can never go away until one discovers the truth." Charlie took her daughter's hand in hers. "That's exactly how I feel too dear." Just then, Annie put her head around the door, saying that as most of the clearing up had been done, Bob was ready to drive them all home now.

As it was still only around 9.30pm and everything was running smoothly, Corinne remained sitting in the lounge in contemplative mood, as there was now so much to think about. She'd resisted the temptation to go and help out in the bar and somehow was not quite ready to go up to her apartment and close the door on the day.

"Do you mind if I join you?" a voice with clearly a Canadian accent asked. Corinne looked up and into the eyes of Jonathan Meyer, now hovering in the doorway with what was clearly a chunky guidebook in his hand. "No, not at all, do come in," said Corinne, already in manager mode and getting hurriedly to her feet. "Oh! please don't get up on my account," replied Jonathan, advancing into the room and taking the other leather armchair opposite and putting his guidebook down on a nearby coffee table. "Are you staying here too?" he asked conversationally.

"Well, sort of because I am Corinne Potter, the manager," she replied, getting up and coming across to shake hands.

"I'm Jonathan Meyer and I arrived this afternoon with my parents, who've already gone up because they're pretty tired from all the driving we've done today. Might you join me for a nightcap. If you're allowed to imbibe on duty that is?"

In a flash, Corinne was remembering all her mother had eventually told her about being dazzled and willingly seduced by one Brad Meyer, also from Toronto in Bristol's Star Hotel a lifetime ago. She hesitated. Here was the perfect opportunity to find out all about the Meyers. "That's very kind of you so what would you like?" she asked.

Her thoughts were in turmoil as she stepped behind the bar.

Yes, Charlie was right. Something really weird was going on because literally a few minutes after promising to find out what she could about the Meyers, Jonathan had walked in and, like her mother in the Star Hotel, she found his soft Canadian accent and gentle manner unnervingly attractive.

"There appeared to be quite a party going on in that big house across the way when we arrived this afternoon," he remarked, accepting his coffee liquor and placing it on the table beside his book. The party, Corinne explained, had been to celebrate her mother's 75th birthday and that Albany House was where her sister Laura lived with her husband Ben and family.

"He runs the Old Mill House Visitors' Centre and Craft Workshops, which you would have passed on coming into the village and would be well worth a visit before you leave," she suggested. "So, what brings you and your parents to Little Oreford?" she asked, although, of course, she already knew the answer to her question.

Jonathan told how he and his father Martin and mother Karen, had traced his great, great grandfather William's roots back to a small picturesque town called Zaandam in The Netherlands, their first stop after flying into Amsterdam three weeks ago.

"It was while we were there that we were able to confirm that his ancestors later moved over the channel to England and settled in North Devon, before eventually emigrating to Canada at the beginning of the 19th Century," he explained.

"It's amazing that you should have been able to find out so much in such a short time," said Corinne. "Oh, not really, because we haven't done all the research ourselves," admitted Jonathan. "When my parents said they wanted to find out about our family past before it was too late, I knew I'd never have the time, or indeed the inclination, to do the research, so I did what I normally do in such situations, in that I just hired an expert to do the job. Esther was good, albeit pretty expensive, and it took her some time, but eventually she came up with our ancestral road map from Europe to Canada and made all the appointments with the people we'd need to see along the way, and we've just been following it, so it's as simple as that," he explained. "How amazing! So, who have you got to meet around here?"

she asked. "Ah, now therein lies a small snag because all our researcher was able to find out was that one Jan Meyer and his family settled in a parish called St Mary's in North Devon for around eighty years, before finally emigrating to Canada." He paused and sipped his coffee. "Now there are quite a few churches called St Mary's around these parts in places like Bideford and Totnes, and just down the road in Hampton Green.
"So tomorrow we're off to Totnes, to begin poking around the churchyard looking for clues on the gravestones."

Corinne wondered why on earth they weren't starting in Hampton Green first in case it proved to be the one, but kept the thought to herself. "You're in for a treat then because those are all lovely old places to visit," she said, asking Jonathan if she could get him another drink. "Perhaps a small brandy this time and for you," he invited. Corinne naturally wanted to continue their conversation, so said she'd join him as she was off duty. 'Now there's a most attractive woman,' thought Jonathan as he watched her return to the bar. Corinne too felt her temperature rising as her thoughts flashed back to her mum and Brad making their way up to his room, where they both knew what was going to happen! 'But that's not going to be happening to me, at least not tonight,' she told herself. "So, finding the North Devon village where your ancestors came from and then delving back into old parish records really is the last piece in the jigsaw," said Corinne, after they'd both settled back in their chairs and 'chinked' glasses. "That's right, Esther tried to access records from our side of the pond, but it wasn't proving that simple, so I decided it would be a great thing for us to do, while visiting some lovely old English towns and villages in the process. And we've certainly struck lucky on that account with Little Oreford," he said.

Corinne was now really tempted to reveal that her own father was called Meyer and by some amazing coincidence, he was also from Toronto, but if she did that, then the whole family story would come tumbling out and it was far too late for that now.

No, she'd wait and discuss the situation with Laura first.

"Time to retire I think, so what time do you serve breakfast?" asked Jonathan as he emptied his glass.

Chapter 3

It had been arranged in a hurried conversation with Laura and Ben, before Corinne and Charlie had gone back to the inn, that they'd meet up in Ben's office over at the Old Mill around 11am the following morning to discuss the new Jameson Family Trust Fund.
Corinne hadn't slept well. She'd deliberately arranged to have the morning after the party off, which was just as well, because what with the surprise trust fund proposal and thinking about Johnathan Meyer, and maybe going off to Canada in search of her father, her mind went into overdrive the minute her head hit the pillow. She'd eventually fallen asleep around 3.30am, so it was gone 9.30am by the time she'd showered and dressed and emerged into yet another warm and sunny morning.
It had almost reached the point where she was longing for rain, at least enough to revive the parched village green, which had developed network of cracks, the like of which she'd never seen before. Corinne just caught sight of the Meyers driving off as she walked across the cobbled stable yard to the inn, picking up an empty pint glass and an ash tray overflowing with cigarette buts from one of the tables as she did so. It caused her a moment of intense annoyance that her staff had clearly

failed to follow a long-established house rule that all public areas in and around the inn should be left clean and tidy before anyone went home. Glasses left out overnight and there for all the guests to see in the morning were a sure sign of a lazy operation and a slipping of standards, and that she would not tolerate. Suddenly in inspection mode, she made a snap tour of all the public toilets to make sure they were spotless and supplied with fresh towels and that all the soap dispensers had been refilled, and luckily, for the person responsible, they were.

Fresh coffee was brewing on the hot plate in the corner of Ben's office, when Corinne arrived to find both he and Laura already seated and in the middle of a row, which cut off the minute she opened the door. That was a surprise because rowing was something Ben and her sister hardly ever did.

"Before we start discussing the trust fund, I have some other interesting news to share with you," she announced while pouring herself a coffee. Now she had their full attention.

"You know our father's name was Meyer and that he was a businessman from Toronto. Well, three guests called Meyer checked in while we were all at the party yesterday and, according to Annie, who was on reception at the time, they were also from Toronto," she told them. "That is interesting news," agreed Ben. "So, do we know anything more about these guests?" he asked. "As a matter of fact, we do, because mum naturally made the connection immediately after being told of their arrival by Annie when she joined us at the party.

She broke the news to me when we went back to the inn, while you were clearing up, and asked me to try and find out if we might just all be related in some way," she explained.

"This all sounds rather intriguing, so go on," invited Ben.

"Just after Bob and Annie had collected mum, I was still sitting in the residents' lounge, when Jonathan Meyer, the son, actually put his head around the door and came and joined me!"

Corinne told them all about the Meyers and how she'd stopped short of revealing their father's name was also Meyer because it was getting late and she wanted to consult them first.

"The chances are there's no connection because Canada's a huge country and these Meyers emigrating from England could have gone anywhere, and it would be a sheer fluke if they ended up in Toronto," Ben rationalized. "Still, it would be interesting to find out where they settled," he conceded. Laura was not quite so sure it was worth raking up the past all over again. "So, getting back to the trust fund, have you two had any initial thoughts on all this overnight?" Corinne asked brightly. "We have, but to tell you the truth, we're not exactly seeing eye to eye at the moment," admitted Ben, looking across at Laura and smiling weakly. 'So that's what the raised voices were all about,' thought Corinne. "Yes, Ben's all for going full-steam ahead on some new projects, while I think it would be nice if he took some time off and we started doing more things together, especially as we'll now have the funds to employ a part time assistant," she said flatly, looking across at Laura for some sisterly support.

It was at times like these, not that there were many of them, when Corinne questioned whether she really needed a man in her life to complicate things.
She'd also inherited her mother's instinct for coming up with inspirational solutions and acting on them and one suddenly popped into her head. "So, here's how we achieve the best of both worlds," she announced, grabbing their full attention.

"The Oreford has been doing really well over the past couple of years, so much so, that we have a more than healthy bank balance," she revealed.

"The team I have in place at the moment, with Annie as my deputy and Andy, who runs the whole catering operation with efficiency and flare, means that I too could take some real time off." Now both Laura and Ben were beginning to wonder where, exactly, this conversation was going.

"I do plan to take an extended break, but even so, I would not be completely at ease and resisting the temptation to keep in regular touch, unless I knew someone was still in overall charge, and I would be really happy if that was you, Ben.

The business could easily afford to pay you a manger's salary for just popping in every now and again to liaise with Annie and to ensure that all was on track. This would allow you to employ an assistant here, without breaking in to the new trust fund, and take a lot more time off to spend with Laura and then maybe the two of you could take on the fund as a joint project."

Laura suddenly surprised herself by brightening up at the prospect. It was as if in that moment, she'd faced up to the fact that since the kids had left home, she'd become rudderless, but had been in denial and had devoted more and more of her time helping Lottie with the twins. But Jack and Hannah had recently started school over at Hampton Green and Lottie had followed in her footsteps by becoming a part-time member of the team at Randall's during school hours, so she'd suddenly found herself at a completely loose end and wanting to spend more time with Ben. "Corinne, you're a genius. I think that's a great Idea!" she said. Ben, seeing the spark of enthusiasm in his wife's eyes, could not help but agree. "But where will you go on your extended holiday?" Laura questioned.

"I accept Ben's point that these Meyers could have settled anywhere in Canada, but now this has all come up, I think I will fly over there and see what I can find out."

Reacting to the surprised look on their faces, Corinne told them how Jonathan Meyer had hired this researcher to help discover their European roots, so perhaps she could also engage her to trace the Meyer family. "But surely you could do that with a phone call rather than going out there," Laura pointed out. "Yes, I could, but Canada is one of the many places on my bucket list and it would be much more interesting to go out there with a purpose," she replied. "Can't argue with that," chipped in Ben. "So as long as you've both got no objections, I thought I'd tell Jonathan about our family background, made all the more intriguing because we share the same surname and that our dad was also from Toronto."

Laura picked up instantly that Mr Meyer had suddenly become 'Jonathan' and wondered if her sister was attracted to him.

Not unsurprisingly, she too was suddenly thinking about the night Brad Meyer had swept their mother off her feet and made her pregnant with the pair of them. "This is turning out to be quite a meeting, so what are we going to do about this £1.5 million that has suddenly landed in our laps?" asked Ben. "Now that is really going to give us something to think about husband," Laura replied.

Chapter 4

Corinne was behind reception and watching out for Jonathan to return from Totnes so she could invite him to join her for a coffee or a drink later, but her plans were suddenly pre-empted by a surprise invitation.
She was in the middle of reading a new menu that Andy had left with her, when a discreet cough diverted her attention, and there was Jonathan and his parents, standing expectantly in front of her. "We wondered if you might care to join us for dinner tonight," say around 7.30pm," he suggested. "I'd be delighted. I've been manager here for a few years now and that's the first invitation I've ever received from a guest," she told them. Feeling a pleasant tingle of anticipation, she returned to her apartment to change and redo her make up. She'd already decided not to give her team advance warning that they'd be serving the boss because it would be interesting to see how they responded.
Word that Corinne was dining with 'those Canadian guests' reached Andy in the kitchen almost immediately after the party had settled down around the corner table, she'd chosen as the most private in the restaurant. Luckily his 'whites' were still fresh, it being so close to the start of service, so he asked Florence, their regular

Sunday evening waitress, to ask 'the boss' if she'd like him come out and guide her guests through the 'specials.' This suggestion, which Florence made to Corinne as discreetly as she could, took her by surprise. "Yes, do ask Andy to come out," she replied, feeling her team had rather turned the tables on her. "Andy is my sister Laura's son-in-law. He's married to her daughter Lottie, my niece, and they have five-year-old twins," Corinne explained after he'd returned to the kitchen and Florence had taken their orders.

During the dinner, she learned that Jonathan and his parents lived together in a fine old detached house in down town Toronto's Rosedale neighbourhood, one of the oldest suburbs in the city and that father and son ran a law firm.

"It was established by my father, Joe Meyer, after returning from serving as a radio officer with the Canadian Air Force, based at RAF Acklington, near a place called Amble in Northumberland," explained Martin. "We thought of paying it a visit until we learned it closed in 1975 and that the main camp was now a prison." Corinne seized the moment. This was the perfect opportunity to raise the subject that had been foremost in her mind since they'd all sat down together.

"All this talk about discovering your roots has really set me thinking, because your arrival here in Little Oreford can only be described as a huge coincidence," she replied, pausing for effect. "You're never going to believe this, but my father was one Brad Meyer, also from Toronto, who to put it quite bluntly, got my student mother pregnant with my sister and I during a one-night stand in Bristol, before flying home and never being heard of again." It was if a time bomb, that had been quietly ticking away for a life-time, had suddenly exploded in their midst and was followed by a stunned silence as Martin put down his knife and fork and looked at her.

"That's simply staggering," he said, now glancing at Jonathan and his wife, whose faces were wearing masks of incredulity.

"This really can't be happening, can it, Karen?" he uttered.

Corinne had expected a surprised reaction, but nothing like this and then it dawned on her that they actually knew who Brad Meyer was. "Oh dear. I hope I haven't spoken out of turn," she said, trying in some way to retrieve the situation.

"Of course, you haven't my dear," said Jonathan's father quietly.

"But you'll see how shocked we all are at your news when I tell you that Brad Meyer was my Uncle Frank's son, which makes you and Jonathan here, cousins," he revealed.

"Brad disappeared somewhere in Central America in the late 1960s, possibly in the same year that he visited Bristol."

Now it was Corinne's turn to be blown away by the shock wave she'd so unwittingly unleashed. She glanced at her watch. It was just after 9pm.

"Do you mind if I give my sister a quick call and ask her and Ben and my nephew Luke to join us, because I really can't wait a moment longer to break the news to them."

Hurrying towards reception, the thought flashed into her head that it might not be OK to have a relationship with one's cousin. She noticed that a large circular table on the far side of the restaurant was now vacant and had been cleared so would be ideal for all of them.

Laura and Ben were in the middle of a discussion about the family development fund and how 'Uncle Robin' had his eye on the derelict kennels, when the phone rang.

"Laura, drop everything and get over here with Ben and bring Luke if he's around," she urged.

"What on earth's up?" she asked catching the excitement in her sister's voice. "We're very closely related to the Meyers," was all she would say before ringing off.

Ten minutes later, after they'd all gathered around the table and the introductions had been made, Corinne broke the news. "You're never going to believe this, but Martin's late Uncle Frank had an only son, Brad, who flew off to Central America on a business trip in the late 1960s and disappeared," she revealed, registering the look of amazement on her twin's face.

"So, do you know why he went off?" asked Ben, once everyone had started coming to terms with the extraordinary situation.

Martin, now holding his wife's hand, as it was resting on the table, said that perhaps it was time he told the whole family story.

"My father, Joe Meyer, and his brother, my Uncle Frank, were partners in Joseph B Meyer, which stood for Brian, the law firm, which my father established, after his return from serving with The Royal Canadian Airforce in WW2," he told them.

"My uncle married Jane, a student, whom he met at college, and they had Brad nine months later. Brad, always brilliant with figures, even as a young lad, could astound the family by adding up enormous sums in his head. So it was not surprising that after graduating from university with honours in accountancy, he found his way into international finance and starting flying all over the world doing investment deals of one sort or another. This was probably why he was in Bristol and met your mum all those years ago," he reasoned.

"But while he was outwardly charming and immediately hit it off with most everyone he met, he also had a very private and secretive side to him, especially about his business interests," Martin revealed.

"He operated out of an apartment in Toronto's business district and rarely kept in touch with my uncle, sometimes going for months without contacting any of the family, which was most upsetting. Anyway, he did drop in to see both his father and my uncle in the office on that last rare occasion and, to put it bluntly, they had a falling out. It appears to have been over a suggestion that some of his dealings were now sailing a little too close to the wind and could possibly tarnish the family firm's impeccable reputation. The Toronto business community, like many others around the world, is quite close-knit at its core and word does get around, especially as most business and financial deals have a contractual and therefore legal aspect to them.

It was shortly afterwards, that he flew off to Costa Rica, having said he might be away for a while, but was never heard from again. After he'd gone more than his usual period of staying out of touch, my uncle, who was not in good health, made a number of attempts to find out what happened to him, but all to no avail so he just gave up in the end," he explained.

"That's awful," broke in Corinne, now beginning to wonder just what had happened to her father and feeling a sadness for her grandfather.

"My uncle eventually got the authority to sell Brad's apartment and gathered up all his personal belongings and papers and stored them in a trunk in his loft. When he and my Aunt Jane died, my father Joe took possession of the trunk.

Then, when he and my mother had passed, I transferred it to my loft, where it has remained ever since."

A hushed silence fell over the gathering, broken only by the background noise from the surrounding tables, as Martin paused, considering what to say next.

"I guess that as his daughters, you and your mother now have the right to know what is inside the trunk, but to be perfectly honest with you, I'd prefer to let the past remain in the past."

Laura was the first to respond.

"You need never have told us about the trunk, seeing how you feel about It, but you did and I for one have no desire to go against your wishes. What do you think Sister?"

Corinne nodded in agreement, but wasn't quite so sure how she felt.

"I'll tell you something," interjected Ben, as if, attempting, to lighten the mood of the gathering. "Corinne is also brilliant with figures, which is why she handles all the finances for the inn and our Old Mill House and Heritage Centre and Craft Workshops. But I guess the most important thing to be done now is to break the news to your mum."

Chapter 5

"My this is some place," Jonathan remarked approvingly as they swept along the drive to pull up outside Little Oreford Court with Corinne and Laura just in front.
It had been agreed the previous evening, that the Meyers would spend the morning visiting St Mary's Church in Hampton Green, so they'd be available to call on Charlie in the afternoon if that was convenient for her. Corinne had driven straight over to break the news to her mum, immediately after the last overnight guest had checked out and was alone because Laura had a hairdressing appointment she did not want to miss.
"Something inside me just knew we were going to be related," said Charlie, after Corinne had poured out the whole remarkable story. "I know Mum because you told me so, and gave me your blessing to go and find my father, and from what we were told last night, it seems he just disappeared off to Costa Rica and was never heard from again."
Corinne hesitated, wondering whether she should voice the thought that had just popped into her head, but Charlie got there first. "So might it be that he did truly intend sending for me, but something awful happened, which caused him to disappear and forget all about me,

and I have been thinking the worst of him for all these years." Charlie bit her lip as a single tear escaped onto her cheek. "Oh Mum, now I have all the more reason to go and find out the truth!" she said, drawing close and giving her a heartfelt hug. "Yes, you do my darling," said Charlie, drying her eyes with a tissue.

After Corinne had gone and she'd recovered her composure from the initial shock, Charlie found herself feeling a calming sense of detachment. It was a trait of her character which had always supported her generally optimistic view on life.

The following sunny morning passed in a flash, and now she was standing hesitantly in the court's grand entrance portico wondering just how she should greet her guests. She watched as, emerging from his car, Jonathan turned and waited for his parents. Now he was walking towards her and she saw in an instant that he looked so like Brad, whose young fresh-faced features had remained indelibly etched on her memory for a life time. "I think this is too precious a moment for formal handshakes," she said, stepping forward and hugging him. Then she turned and embraced Martin and Karen, who were standing slightly awkwardly behind him.

"Come in, come in," she invited, leading the way into her lavishly furnished low oak-beamed lounge, where soft side lights in the darker corners competed with the bright afternoon sunlight, streaming in though leaded windows. Once they were all seated, Charlie relived the happy day she'd spent with Brad. She recalled how she'd collected him from Bristol's Star Hotel and acted as his tour guide around the former maritime city before returning to the hotel for dinner and then on to bed. It was best they knew the whole story she'd decided. So, she told of his promise to send her air tickets to join him in Toronto, just as soon as he got home. But they'd never arrived, and how weeks later she'd discovered she was pregnant with twins, whom she'd reluctantly given up for adoption, only to be reunited with many years later.

"I was telling your daughters earlier, that while I never really had anything to do with Brad, I got the impression that my cousin was quite a principled person and not the sort to make promises to you he had not fully intended keeping, and that maybe something happened, which suddenly took him away from us all," said Martin. A hush fell over the room as everyone absorbed the significance of those few words and of the mystery they now presented. Confirmation that Brad was not the sort to make false promises, was having a profound effect on Charlie, who was now re-evaluating her feelings and coming to terms with the fact that he may not have enticed her into bed with absolutely no intention of it going any further. 'But be honest Charlie, he never enticed you because you were as keen to make love to him as he was to you,' she told herself.

Now Martin was saying that, as they'd found the family, they never knew they had, the need to go on researching their roots seemed to have completely lost its significance. "We set out searching for our past and have ended up finding our present," he said. There was a sudden commotion as Lottie, having left work at Randall's and picked up her twins, arrived and was introduced to the relations, who'd not existed until a few hours earlier. "I think this amazing reunion calls for another celebration dinner party," announced Charlie, regaining her previous ascendency over the conversation. "But first I think it's time for tea," she said, suddenly spotting Annie hovering in the doorway with a large silver tray, which she carried carefully into the room and set out on a nearby highly polished walnut table. "Yours is a familiar face," said Jonathan suddenly catching her eye.

"That's right and it's because I checked you in the other afternoon," she explained, smiling back at him. "Yes Jonathan, you'll soon learn, if you haven't already, that we're one big extended family around here, because

Annie and her husband Bob are close friends and have the apartment above the old stable block," explained Charlie.

The gathering broke up an hour later with it being arranged that they'd all return to Charlie's for an early supper the following Saturday, which would allow Martin, Karen and Jonathan another three clear days to compete their tour around North Devon.

Once the Meyers had departed and Laura had gone off to help Lottie get the twin's tea, Corinne sat down for a heart-to-heart with her mum and to talk over all that had happened over the past couple of days. "To think it was only at your party you suggested that Laura and I should go off and find Brad, Mum and now look what's happened. It's comforting after all these years, to hear from Martin that our father was not the kind of man to make promises he didn't intend keeping, so is that enough to finally close the book on this now do you think?" asked Corinne. "I don't know dear. It's all been such a lot to take in, so I'm not sure how I feel at the moment. Maybe you should ask Jonathan what he thinks you should do," Charlie suggested. "Yes, that's a good idea," agreed Corinne suddenly glimpsing the tantalising possibility of her and Jonathan flying off to Costa Rica together.

It didn't matter how old or sensible one was, when it came to the sudden prospect of a romance with someone you really fancied, most normal everyday people could still suddenly find themselves in first date mode, she thought.

"I'm just going upstairs to fetch something," said Charlie, getting slowly to her feet. There was a faraway look in her eyes. She returned a few minutes later with a small jewellery box and placed it on the coffee table in front of them. "Open it dear," she instructed. Corinne raised the tiny lid to reveal a silver St Christopher on a chain. "That was a little gift bought for me by your father on our day out together and somehow, despite everything, I've never had the heart to part with it. So, if you do go off to find your father, and by some miracle, and goodness knows this family has had more than its fair share of those, he is still alive, then this will be all the proof you'll need for him to know that you are indeed his daughter."

When Corinne got back to the inn, she spotted the Meyers in the restaurant, but decided it would be far better to leave them in peace. She'd opt instead for a quiet evening, having an early bath, making some supper and curling up in front of the telly in her dressing gown. The television had just gone on when her internal phone rang and she picked it up to hear Alice's voice.

"Sorry to disturb, but I have Mr Jonathan Meyer here wanting to know if you might be free to join him for a nightcap in the residents' lounge. Her heart leapt, but no she would decline the invitation because the prospect of throwing on her clothes, hurriedly putting on her makeup and rushing downstairs was all too much to contemplate. "Do tell Mr Meyer that I've already turned in for the night, but would be happy to join him tomorrow evening, say around 9pm if he was free.

Turning back to the telly she half watched a drama until the news came on.

But being suddenly confronted by disturbing scenes of prolonged droughts in Africa and starving, fly infested children, she switched it off and went to bed. 'I wonder if Luke's been watching that,' was her last thought before sleep overwhelmed her.

Corinne normally woke well before 7am, but it was getting on for 9am when the phone eventually woke her. It was Laura calling and there was excitement in her voice. "Ben and I have been kicking around lots of ideas about the development fund so would you like to pop over for supper say around 7pm?" Her thoughts immediately zeroed in on her date with Jonathan, but reckoned that two hours would be plenty long enough to talk over development fund ideas before making her excuses and leaving, so she agreed.

She found her sister more animated than she'd seen her for a long time. The whole development fund idea had certainly brought her out of some gloomy place and it was clear that it had also had some restorative effect on Ben too. The contrast in her sister's outlook suddenly made Corinne feel guilty that she'd been so wrapped up in running the inn, that she'd been too busy to think about them. The fact that they'd been struggling to make ends meet with the mill, while having to support their lives at Albany House, had passed her by and made her feel even more uncomfortable, especially as The Oreford had been doing so well of late. Still if she did fly off in search of Brad, then she'd make sure the salary she paid Ben to keep an eye on the inn, would be more than enough to make a real difference.

"We've gone off Uncle Robin's idea of restoring the old kennels because we can't see a way to make any income from them and think it would become a drain on our resources," said Laura.

"But Lottie told us in passing that a new instruction came in to Randall's yesterday for the sale of quite a large house not far from here on the Draymarket Road. So we thought it could be ideal for a luxury bed and breakfast business," she explained.

"We could use it as an alternative offering when the inn is full and it would almost certainly generate additional lunches and dinners for you, as well as more business for the mill," pointed out Ben. "It would also provide more local employment opportunities, which heaven knows, we could do with around here," he added. "That sounds a great idea," Corinne agreed. "But perhaps we could just do something with the old kennels to give Uncle Robin a hands-on involvement, because, after all, we mustn't forget that he and Auntie Margo are actually the founders of our family feast," she pointed out.

Corinne managed to slip away just before 9pm and found Jonathan already sitting in the lounge and mid-way through a novel. "So what's your taste in reading?" she asked. He looked up and smiled at her. "I mostly read biographies, but I can get into the occasional thriller series if something grabs me," he replied. "I'll just pop into the bar for a glass of wine, so can I get you anything else?" she asked, "No. I'm fine at the moment because I'm rather full of one of your Andy's excellent steak pies and had rather more than my share of two bottles of red."

When she returned, they talked over their various doings of the day and she learned that their forays around North

Devon had been delightful, albeit a little on the warm side. But they'd been fruitless as far as the family history was concerned because nothing had come to light in any of the St Mary's churchyards, including the one in Hampton Green.

"To tell you the truth, and as I said when we met your charming mother, finding a close branch of the family we never knew we had, has become rather more important than researching our roots and we're all looking forward to tomorrow evening's dinner party," he said. "You'd better prepare yourself then because the whole clan's going to be there, including our adopted uncle and aunt, Robin and Margo, and several other very close family friends," she explained. "Will we also be seeing the lady, who first checked us in and who served the tea the other afternoon?" asked Jonathan. "Yes. You'll certainly be seeing Annie and her husband Bob. Annie's one of our two duty managers. She became very close to mum when she lived in a retirement hotel in Sidmouth before moving back here a few years ago. Corinne didn't go in to the extraordinary circumstances surrounding Charlie's return because it was all too complicated, but she did want to raise another delicate matter with Jonathan.

"I appreciate how your father feels about Brad's trunk, but if he knew that I really would like to find out what happened to my father, do you think he might change his mind?" she asked. "I don't know, but I guess it's up to you to ask him."

Chapter 6

Martin Meyer was polite, but Corinne was left in little doubt that he was still uncomfortable with the idea, and a few days later, the Meyer's flew back to Toronto, but not before contact details had been exchanged and they'd issued an open invitation for everyone to come and visit them that fall.

Corinne felt completely deflated once they'd gone, but decided she should wait at least a couple of days before emailing Jonathan, who'd seemed just the slightest bit remote when everyone had gathered in the car park to say their farewells.

'Oh dear, I do hope history isn't about to repeat itself all over again,' she thought as she went back inside.

Laura and Ben were now in acquisition mode over the upmarket B&B project, but somehow, she couldn't bring herself to share their enthusiasm, and that only served to heighten the sense of loneliness, which had now stolen over her.

It was a couple of days before Jonathan responded to her email, saying that his father was unwell following the flight home, but even then, his note wasn't particularly warm and friendly, not in the way they'd been in one another's company.

One evening when things had quietened down, she found herself sitting in the armchair he'd occupied in the residents' lounge as if she was trying to somehow reignite the spark of warmth that had been between them in that small space. It was strange to think that she was now experiencing something of the feeling of loss that her mum must have felt as she waited and waited to hear from Brad.

'But at least I'm not pregnant,' she told herself, hurriedly getting up as if trying to leave her morose self still sitting there. Then an idea that had been vaguely in her thoughts for a couple of days, like a quiet tapping on a door, came in to her mind.

If Ben and Laura's, now mega plan, to direct more business to the mill and the inn by setting up, not just one, but a small chain of satellite up-market B&B operations around Little Oreford, was going ahead, then what she was going to need, was a large conservatory extension. She'd actually needed it for quite a while now, as the business had flourished, thanks to Andy's culinary expertise, and it could be an extension out from the restaurant into the stable yard, she told herself.

Corinne retired to her apartment feeling a whole lot better having kickstarted herself out of the mildly depressive mood that had been prevailing ever since the Meyers had left, and fell into a deep sleep.

She'd previously declined Laura's invitation to accompany her and Ben on a second viewing of Rose Cottage, but called saying she'd changed her mind, and would meet them there around 11am, because she was going on in to Draymarket for lunch with her close friend Alicia, afterwards. She'd half expected it would be her niece Lottie, now wearing her Randall's estate agency hat, who'd be showing them around, but no, it was Heather Brooks, the other half of 'The Demons' duo, who with her partner Hannah, usually dominated the pub quiz at The Lion in Hampton Green. Corinne went to the quiz about once a month and had long ago learned to live with the friendly jibes from the regulars that she was only there to see what the opposition was up to.

Both Heather and Hannah, who ran their own B&B business in a converted barn close to the pub, were now semi-retired, having worked with Royston Randall for many years, first together with him in the Hampton Green agency, and later as he expanded his operation first into Draymarket and then right across the county.

"They're a bit short staffed at Hampton so Royston called to ask if I'd pop into the office, pick up the keys from Lottie and come on over," Heather told them.

"That's a bit of a coincidence because I'm meeting Alicia later for lunch," said Corinne who'd become close friends with Royston and his wife after they became regular diners at The Oreford.

Rose Cottage with its four double bedrooms, large enough to accommodate en-suits, good size kitchen and lounge-diner and pleasant gardens looking out over open country would be ideal for their purposes, so they'd be making an offer, Ben told Hannah at the end of the viewing.

Alicia Randall, now in her early forties, was still a very attractive woman, being slim and fair with delicate features and extremely well dressed, as became a wealthy estate agent's wife. She was already occupying their reserved table at the small Italian bistro and former wine bar in the High Street, when Corinne arrived. The two made small talk while ordering sparkling water and studying the menu. "I can't believe how the time has flown, when I think that both Lottie and Luke were in my class at Hampton Junior back in the days when I rented Ben and Laura's old house after they moved up to Little Oreford," she said.

For one uncomfortable moment, her mind threw up the image of jealous psychopath Tanya Talbot poised to murder her and Royston after discovering them together in his bungalow when she'd paid him a surprise visit one evening.

"Have I got some news for you," said Corinne after they'd ordered and handed back their menus. They spent the whole lunchtime discussing the Meyers, and especially Jonathan, and trying to puzzle out why he'd seemingly become remote after they'd appeared to be getting on so well, and might even have ended up in bed together, if he'd given her half a chance.

"I think that asking Martin about finding out what had happened to your dad was the trigger," said Alicia. "They're bound to have discussed it later and I bet Jonathan tried persuading his father to sanction the idea and it ended up in a row," she suggested. "Oh dear. I think you could well be right, but what do I do now?" Alicia thought about this for a moment. "To be honest, I don't think there's anything you can do because if you press the subject with Jonathan, that might push him even further away and that's the last thing you want," she warned.

"I can't pursue it now, but the Meyers have invited us all to go over in October and I think I'll be accepting their invitation," said Corinne. "So, roll on the fall, as they say in Canada" responded Alicia. "Let's drink to that and maybe I could come along too, if you're allowed to bring a friend," she said, raising her glass.

"Now that's not a bad idea because Ben's already agreed to keep an eye on the inn while I have a holiday and Laura certainly wouldn't go without him, and I can't really see mum wanting to jet off to Toronto, although I'd wouldn't put it past her," she smiled.

"But being serious for a moment, I think I'd feel a bit vulnerable turning up at the Meyers all by myself, not quite knowing what sort of reception to expect from Jonathan, but if you came too, it would change the dynamics completely and we could have a great holiday together, even if nothing more was ever said about finding out what happened to Brad." She paused, turning the delightful prospect over in her mind. "But do you think Royston would mind if you did come out with me?" she asked. "Oh, I don't really think so because, apart from having the business to totally absorb him, he'd probably spend most of his weekends with his new best buddy Mark Hammond, chairman of their classic and vintage car club." Corinne looked up at her friend. "Do I sense a little discontentment here Alicia?" she probed. "No, not really Corinne because Royston works such long hours that who am I to give him a hard time when it comes to his precious cars?" she rationalised. "Isn't Mark the rather dishy one we met at your last soiree?"

she asked. "Yes, I suppose you could call him that," she admitted, "He'd be a great catch for someone because he's something to do with one of the leading hedge funds in the city and seems to be loaded."

They parted in the bistro's small car park behind the premises.

'Yes, it would be great to get away with Corinne for a couple of weeks in the autumn, Alicia thought as she began the short drive home. And yes, Royston's often taking her for granted was beginning to get her down, she admitted to herself.

"Royston darling, what would you say if I went off with Corinne to Toronto for two or three weeks, say in October?" asked Alicia, after she'd spent most of their evening meal telling him all about the Meyers and Brad. "Anthony will be back at boarding school and I'm sure you could manage without me," she said, giving him one of her gentle smiles, that had always captivated him.

"Oh! I'm not so sure about that," he said, while actually thinking it might be quite nice to have a little time all to himself for the first time in years. "No, seriously, I think it's a great idea darling," he said, rising to clear the dinner table.

When Corinne got back, she went straight over to Albany House to discuss her plan with Laura, who was happy to go along with it, although still not really sure that searching for Brad was a good idea. "I don't know why, but I just have an uncomfortable feeling that somehow no good will come of it," she said. "Look sister dear, I'm not going to push the idea, especially as we now know that Jonathan's father is not at all keen, so Alicia and I will just be having a great girlie holiday together," she reassured Laura.

Back in her apartment and on her laptop, Corinne Googled the time difference between the UK and Toronto, wondering if this might be the right time to actually call Jonathan. It was now 4pm and 9pm on the other side of the pond, so was that too late to call or should she wait until tomorrow? No. She didn't want to wait so she'd call him now. The phone seemed to go on ringing and ringing until an answerphone kicked in notifying callers this was the Meyers' residence, but unfortunately no one could come to the phone just now. So, should she leave a message? Corinne agonised for a second or two, but then put the phone down feeling suddenly deflated. She tried again at 3pm the following afternoon and again no one was at home, but this time she did leave a message.

This was all really weird because she knew she was experiencing the same cocktail of emotions that her mum must have felt when her father had not returned her calls a life-time ago.

It was right in the middle of a busy lunch time service a couple of days later, when she was helping out in the restaurant, that Annie, on reception, picked up the call from Jonathan and came out to find her. Corinne felt a sudden surge of excitement!

"Tell him I'm really busy right now and would it be OK if I called him back at 9pm his time?" Annie put the phone down having been told this evening would be fine. So perhaps she'd been right and that her boss could have finally found her man.   That afternoon, Corinne drove over to Little Oreford Court to spend a couple of hours with Charlie and was surprised to meet her nephew, Luke, just leaving. He and his grandmama, were particularly close, although she naturally saw far more of her niece Lottie and the twins. "And how are you today, Mum?" she asked brightly, having found her in her favourite armchair in the lounge with a pile of discarded papers and magazines scattered all around her. "Luke and I have just been having the most fascinating discussion about just what would happen if, during some future winter, the entire country was suddenly hit by a series of violent and prolonged snow storms with temperatures dropping well below zero for weeks on end." Corinne smiled to herself as her nephew had clearly been up on his climate soapbox again, but then chastised herself for being so judgemental.

"He believes it would be a catastrophe because we're now all so dependent on electricity for heating and the internet and just in time deliveries by road to all our supermarkets," said Charlie.

He believes blizzard conditions for days on end would bring down power lines, completely block hundreds of roads and railway lines and that within a week or two, millions of people, especially in the cities, would be left without food or heat and that could result in a complete breakdown of law and order," she added. "That's all a bit dramatic isn't it Mum?" Corrine suggested.

"I suppose, it might be, but you know Luke takes the future of the earth and the fact that global warming is nearing the point of no return, extremely seriously and rightly so."

What she did not tell Corinne, because she felt it wasn't her place to do so, was that having broken up with his long suffering partner, who'd finally given up on his being ready to get married and start a family, he now had a new woman in his life. He'd been in the new relationship with Roxanne, a fellow climate change activist, for six months or so, but had been reluctant to bring her home to meet the family because, besides being extremely alternative, she was also quite outspoken. "Talking about a change of climate, I'm going to have a change of scene by flying off to Toronto to stay with the Meyers and possibly to start trying to find out just what happened to Brad, if you're still happy for me to do that," Corrine announced. "And what's more, my friend Alicia Randall is coming with me," she added.

"I'm delighted because you really do deserve a holiday and I'd come with you both if I felt I was up to travelling, but sadly I don't think I would be these days," she admitted.

"As far as your father is concerned, I don't really mind either way now, but will you at least let me pay for your flights?" Corinne said that was very generous of her, but not necessary and that she'd be calling Jonathan later to make all the arrangements.

The phone only rang for a few moments before she heard his voice and was relieved that it had lost that certain edge she'd detected when they'd parted in the inn car park those few short weeks ago, but her instincts told her that something still wasn't quite right.

"I'm sorry I didn't pick up on your earlier calls and the reason was that my father has died. He developed a deep vein thrombosis on the flight home, followed by further complications and all was compounded by an already weakened heart," he explained.

"Oh Jonathan, I'm so, so, sorry and I know everyone here will be too because we all had such a happy time together."

They talked for a while about his life and about how Jonathan would now be taking overall charge of Joseph B Meyer, a position his father had passionately guarded, even though, in reality, it had been Jonathan, who'd been gradually assuming more and more of the responsibilities within their law firm.

"I'm not sure this is really the right time to raise it, but if your invitation to come and stay is still open, then I'd love to fly over in the fall, as you call it, and bring my friend Alicia with me," she said. "That would be wonderful so, of course you must both come. I can show you around our city and we could also drive up to our camp for a few days hiking and messing about in canoes on the lake if you're up for outdoor pursuits."

Corinne said it sounded wonderful, although there'd never been much time in her life for the great outdoors, while at the same time feeling a twinge of regret that Alicia was now coming too.

Chapter 7

Air Canada flight 617 touched down smoothly just before 8am.

It was a huge relief for Corinne, who'd omitted telling Alicia that, embarrassing as it was, she'd never actually flown before! The whole Heathrow terminal experience had been confusing and disorientating for someone who'd reached early middle age without actually setting foot inside an airport, let alone one of the busiest in the world. But Alicia and Royston were always jetting off with Anthony for long Christmas and New Year breaks in the sun and a couple of shorter ones during the year, so thankfully, she naturally took charge of their check-in.

It didn't take Corinne many moments to spot Jonathan waiting in the arrivals hall, but who was that dishy looking man standing next to him? Abandoning her trolly as he stepped forward to meet her, she gave him a spontaneous hug. It was their first physical contact and just came so naturally. "And this is Alicia," she said stepping back and introducing her friend. "And this is Shaun," Jonathon replied, turning to introduce the slim, blond haired Adonis standing a few feet away. "We're friends and neighbours so he volunteered to drive me this morning because my car started playing up yesterday. It only took a single glance to see that Alicia was impressed.

They all chatted easily on the drive into the city and to Jonathan's home in Rosedale, which both Corinne and Alicia quickly discovered was certainly an affluent and leafy district of large detached mansions.

Jonathan had told her the Meyer practice was one of the most prominent in the city, so the magnificent house they'd just pulled up outside, clearly went with the territory.

Jonathan's mother Karen had heard them coming and was already standing at the top of the steps in the impressive pillared entrance porch to greet them, while Shaun had gone around to his BMW's boot to start retrieving their luggage. "You must be quite tired after your flight, so would you like something to eat or to go to your rooms to rest and freshen up?" she asked after they'd dispensed with the greetings and introductions and Corinne had expressed her sadness at her loss.

"Mother's quite chirpy at the moment because, although the funeral was three weeks ago, I don't think father's not being here anymore has actually sunk in yet," confided Jonathan, as he led the way up a wide staircase and into the first of two large and decidedly chintzy connecting rooms overlooking extensive rear gardens dominated by an ornate pond. "This is really lovely Jonathan," said Corinne, standing in the window. "My Grandfather Joe and Grandma Lizzy had the property built, and it's always been our family home, so I guess I rather take it all for granted," he admitted. "I hope you don't mind because I've invited Shaun over to join us for our traditional brunch around noon as a thank you for this morning," he said as he turned to leave her to unpack, but no sooner had he done so when Alicia entered through their connecting door. "This place is simply amazing and I'm more than glad I came along because I think we're going to have a lovely time," she said, already having noticed that Shaun was not wearing a wedding ring!

"But you've also got a beautiful Victorian home in its own grounds with lovely views," Corinne reminded her. "I know you're right, but I guess, as I overheard Jonathan saying, if you've lived somewhere for a long time, it's so easy to take it for granted."

Brunch wasn't quite the low-key affair Corinne had expected when she and Alicia came downstairs and made their way along a lofty green and white tiled hallway in the direction of what seemed like a lot of voices.

Emerging hesitantly into a large conservatory overlooking the garden, they were confronted by quite a gathering.

"Oh! here are our guests," said Jonathan, turning as if by some natural instinct. "I know this might all seem a little overwhelming, but we've just had a surprise visitation from four very old friends, who happened to find themselves in the area," he said, drawing them into the gathering. They were quickly introduced to the two couples, who'd all been friends with Jonathan since their days at UBC, the university of Vancouver.

The 'getting to know you' ritual continued all over lunch around a long glass topped table and didn't end until getting on for 3pm when the four finally departed and Shaun had also made his excuses and left.

"Might I suggest a relax on the garden loungers because it's still quite warm outside," suggested Jonathan, seeing at a glance that both Corinne and Alicia were flagging and had had almost as much as they could take of being sociable. "Oh yes that would be really great and if it could be accompanied by a large pot of tea, that would be simply wonderful," said Corinne, her mouth suddenly feeling parched, which might be linked to the 'jetlag' she'd head so much about.

But when Jonathan came carefully down the patio steps balancing a large tray a few minutes later, he found them both asleep in the autumn sun. They stirred about an hour later to find their hosts Jonathan and Karen on loungers close by and absorbed in what seemed like a whispered conversation. "I'm so glad you've come back to us because we'd have to have woken you shortly," said Karen brightly. Corinne suddenly caught sight of the abandoned tea tray and felt instantly guilty, as well as thinking she'd like nothing better than to go upstairs right now and sink into bed! Alicia, who didn't feel quite so wacked, could see the effect it was having on her and when Jonathan and his mother went in to make fresh tea, told her the best thing they could do to adjust, would be to fight off the drowsiness and go to bed in Canadian time.

They went up later to get ready for supper and Corinne doused her face in cold water, but it was still almost as much as she could do to come downstairs again. Yet a few minutes later all thoughts of sleep vanished, when Jonathan led them into his book-lined study and towards a table in the window where a leather-bound family photograph album lay closed and ready for inspection. "It only occurred to me on the flight home that, of course, you would never have seen any pictures of your father and that, strangely enough, you'd never asked about that during our stay with you. I had planned to email you some straight away, but then father became ill and all thoughts of doing that were swept aside and then when you said you were coming over, I decided to wait until now."

An odd feeling of detachment settled over Corinne as Jonathan slowly opened the heavy book to a marked page and she stared down and into the face of a young man, probably in his early teens, and holding up a large fish he'd just caught.

"Fishing up at our camp was the only thing that your father and my Great Uncle Frank had in common and was probably because they didn't need to talk much," said Jonathan. But Corinne wasn't really listening. The detachment she'd felt moments earlier was swept away as, gazing down at that fresh face, looking out at her from across the years, she saw how it could so easily have belonged to her! He was not looking particularly happy, as neither she had been during that whole period when she was being shunted between children's homes and foster carers. Never having a father, or a mother, to love and cherish her, had scarred her deeply, but had eventually been buried by the passage of time and her generally optimistic nature. Being reunited with Laura, and later with their mother Charlie, had done much to make her feel whole and complete again, but now looking down into that face belonging to a person who, either by design or accident, had caused so much unhappiness in all of their lives, she decided she really did want to find out what had become of him.

"Sadly, that's the best picture we have of Brad, who appears never to have been one for staring into cameras at the best of times," said Jonathan. Looking up from the page, as if some spell had been broken, Corinne agreed it had been odd that neither she nor Laura had thought to ask about pictures of their father.

"I guess it was because he was a remote figure, who actually meant nothing at all to us, but now seeing his picture and realising that he looks so like me at that age, I can't help having feelings about him," she admitted, her eyes moistening.

"I'm really sorry, I should have guessed that seeing a picture of your father would come as a bit of a shock," apologised Jonathan, leaning forward to close the album. "No don't do that because I haven't finished looking at the picture yet, and you haven't upset me in the least because I would not have missed this moment for the world," replied Corinne, smiling at him weakly.

Standing unobtrusively nearby, was Brad's large and dusty trunk, which Jonathan had eventually found in a dark corner of their extensive loft a couple of days earlier. He'd carefully cleaned it and loosened its rusty straps, and had resisted the temptation of opening it, but this was definitely not the moment to suggest they did so, he decided.

Supper was a quiet affair with just the four of them. They talked over all the events of the last few months and Jonathan laid out his suggested sightseeing plans for the following morning. "I've arranged to take a couple of days off, but that's all I can spare at the moment I'm afraid because of all the changes that are now having to be made following father's passing, but of course you are most welcome to stay for as long as you like."

After supper was over, they both called home. Corinne had decided not to tell Laura she'd seen a picture of Brad, knowing she preferred that he be left buried in the past.

Laura, still buoyant and on a high, thanks to the new sense of purpose in her life, said their offer on Rose Cottage had been accepted and she and Ben were off to view another potential satellite B&B possibility the following afternoon. Corinne was tempted to suggest that perhaps it would be wiser to complete one project before going chasing after another, but then thought better of it.

Ironically, Alicia found herself having a similar conversation with Royston, who was also talking about another possible acquisition. "Surely you don't need any more cars in your collection," she cautioned. "No, my love, not a car, but another business, which I've actually been after for years," he admitted. "But that's your excuse every time and surely the point's going to come when you might think of stopping," she suggested. "Yes, but it's not quite yet," he replied, so completing the little ritual dance they went through every time the Royston Randall chain expanded still further.

Alicia had become bored with her husband, who was totally wrapped up in his prosperous business and his classic car collection, but she adored Anthony, whose sensitive nature mirrored her own. While she fanaticised about taking a lover, there was no way she'd ever seriously contemplate it because of the misery it would cause her son, if it was ever discovered, which being a realist, she knew that eventually, it most probably would.

Jonathan in tourist guide mode, a real novelty for him, suggested their first day's exploration should be a low-key affair because tramping around cities, no matter how exciting and iconic they were, could be exhausting.

They opted instead for a stroll through the parks, a bistro lunch and harbour cruise on Lake Ontario.

Several times during that sunny day, with an autumn crispness in the air, Corinne could not help thinking back to her mum taking Brad on a sightseeing tour around Bristol all those years ago and that how, so weirdly, history was repeating itself.

It was also a day of strangely equal anticipation because while by lunchtime, headstrong Charlie knew instinctively that she'd be ending up in bed with Brad, Corinne was also having similar thoughts. There was also that trunk, which Jonathan had mentioned casually over lunch, was waiting to be opened when they got home, if that was what she wanted.

And that was the question because, despite her earlier resolve to find out what had happened to her father, did she really want it opened after all these years, given Laura's instinctive view that the past should be left buried in the past, because who could tell what dark secrets might come to light. "Once you know something, you can't then unknow it," her twin had said at the time.

"Come back to us," said Alicia gently and half way through the harbour cruise, after she and Jonathan had been making small talk while Corinne gazed out from the rail with a faraway look in her eyes. She'd also been thinking about Jonathan and of the closeness that had been rekindled between them over the past twenty-four hours, and how she'd like to seek him out in his bedroom when all was quiet in the big house, but that would just not seem right with Alicia being around. And then there was the question of why such an attractive man as Jonathan was still single at his age, but then again, so was she!

As it happened, the trunk did not get opened because later that afternoon there was a call from Shaun inviting them around for drinks and a poolside barbecue supper. Shaun Morrison was a self-made man, Jonathan told them on their way home. He was an independent insurance broker specialising mostly in commercial property right across the Americas and had become the go to consultant when it came to obtaining the most advantageous rates and the best prices.

He'd acquired the colonial style house next door to the Meyers some years earlier and his easy manner and charm had quickly made him more than a neighbour and Jonathan's confidant in all matters.

"You're going to be meeting Shaun's family, but they're not the traditional ones," Jonathan explained intriguingly. "They're his live-in housekeeper and cook Lois and his gardener, handyman and occasional chauffer, Lewis, who are both devoted to him. And when I say 'live in' I mean it, because they have the complete run of the house and treat Shaun like the son they never had. "Isn't it all a bit confusing that she's Lois and he's Lewis?" Alicia asked. "No, not really, because we call them Big L and Little L and you'll soon see what I mean," Jonathan replied.

The wafting aroma of slowly cooking food reached them as he led them, not out of the front door, but into the garden and towards an unobtrusive gate in a hedge, which Corinne had half noticed while on her sun lounger the previous afternoon.

"Big L also looks after our grounds, hence the gate," Jonathan explained as he opened it and led them through.

"Oh wow," said Corinne as soon as she caught sight of the oval and marbled swimming pool with two voluptuous and half-naked Greek Goddesses and two similar Venus Adonis standing sentinel around it. "Yes, I know they're quite eye-catching, but I inherited them with the house and I haven't had the heart to get rid of them," explained Shaun, coming forward to greet them.

"Oh! I think it would be a shame to remove them because they are rather magnificent," said Alicia looking at Shaun.

'And you're not so bad yourself,' he thought taking her in approvingly.

Above them on the wide patio, a giant of a man was busily tending the barbecue and close by, a round table laid out for supper, under the shelter of a garden heater. Shaun introduced Lewis, who turned and gave them a wide grin, spatula in hand.

"I hope you're hungry and like steak because these are almost done," he said as Loise, a bubbly personality in her early fifties, came over to meet them.

Five minutes later, they were all sitting around the table filled with bowls of fresh salads.

"This spread is magnificent Shaun," said Alicia, who having already consumed her second glass of good quality sparkling pink Champagne was really beginning to relax and enjoy herself.

"We eat like this most of the time during the summer," don't we Lewis?" The big man nodded, mid mouthful, but made no other comment. For while Shaun regarded them as 'his family,' Corinne noticed they made little attempt to join in the chatter during the supper and only answered as briefly as was polite when brought into the conversation and, as soon as they had eaten, they made their excuses and left.

Corinne and Alicia spent most of the evening answering their host's gently probing questions about their lives, while polishing off a third bottle of full red wine which, as Shaun had said, was an excellent accompaniment to the steak.

"Why haven't you told me all this before Jonathan?" Shaun asked, after Corinne had related the whole Brad story and how she'd eventually found her way to Little Oreford and to the twin sister she never knew she had and how their long-lost mother, Charlie had also turned up some years later.

"Father's death had something to do with that Shaun," he responded, instantly casting a shadow over the table. "Yes, of course. How stupid of me," his friend replied. The embarrassing silence was broken by Alicia asking if that lovely pool was heated. "It's like a warm bath," replied Shaun, happy to have been rescued from the moment. "You're welcome to try it any time while you're here, he invited. "So, what's wrong with the present?" she asked looking at him knowingly. "Nothing really, other than we've been drinking and have eaten quite a lot, but I guess a gentle emersion would probably be OK. So do you want to go and fetch your swimming things if you've brought any?" Shaun asked. "No, not unless you do!" she replied.

She'd never have made so bold had she not been feeling so deliciously light headed. "That's settled then," said Shaun, getting up from the table and walking slowly over to one of the poolside loungers and beginning to undress. Alicia followed, making her way to a lounger on the other side of the pool, while Corinne and Jonathan sat watching their progress. "Do you think we should join them?" he asked quietly.

"It would be rude not to," she replied, feeling her temperature rising as she got to her feet. She took the lounger next to Alicia and also began undressing.

"I can't believe we're doing this," she whispered, but her friend didn't answer and was already lowering herself into the deliciously warm water.

Discovering the pool was only a little over waist deep, she turned and breast stroked towards Shaun, who was already standing in the middle of the pool and watching her. Reaching him, she rose to her feet, her shoulder length blond hair now hanging limp and wet, put her arms around his waist and kissed him gently full on the lips. With that, he brought his arms around her, cupping and gently squeezed her buttocks.

Chapter 8

"You know this can only be a holiday romance, don't you?" said Alicia, resting on one elbow as she casually ran the long fingers of her free hand through the dark mass of hair on Shaun's chest. "Yes, I do know that and I wouldn't have it any other way because my life's full and complicated enough as it is at the moment," he replied, both hands behind his head.
Feeling suddenly reassured, she rolled over on top of him and they began all over again because it was only 6am.
Corinne was still asleep in the big house next door having crept up to bed with Jonathan in the early hours so as not to disturb Karen.
They'd returned soon after 10pm, both eagerly anticipating what was to follow, but really in no hurry, preferring to savour the intimacy that had welled up between them by having a nightcap on the big brown leather Chesterfield sofa in his study.
"I was attracted to you the moment you appeared in the doorway of your residents' lounge, but little could I have dreamt just where it was all going to lead," he said, lifting his small tot of whisky to clink glasses. "It was the same

for me too," she said beginning to feel herself drifting away in a sleepy alcoholic haze.

She woke just after nine with sunlight filtering through the curtains to find herself alone in his king-sized bed while small domestic sounds percolated up from below. She rolled lazily over onto her back. Did she really watch Alicia follow Shaun toward the pool and strip naked before doing so herself and frolicking with Jonathan in the water, which seemed the most natural thing in the world?

The door opening brought her sharply back to the present as Jonathan, attired in a dark blue silk dressing gown, appeared with a breakfast tray.

"Good morning Corrie," because that's what he'd started calling her. "I hope you don't mind me going ahead and getting this?" he said carefully putting the laden tray down on the bedside table on his side. She raised herself up, suddenly feeling slightly awkward by her nakedness, and spotting her bra and underwear uppermost in a jumbled pile of clothes on a chair by the window. Seeing her embarrassment, Jonathan, walked over to a large double wardrobe and quickly found a cherry pink silk dressing gown and bought it over for her. She thanked him and, slipping it on, made her way to the en-suite bathroom to relieve herself and freshen up.

'I wonder who last wore this?' she thought, while sitting there.

"Shaun called earlier, saying that he and Alicia would be around at 11am. He's proposing to treat us all to lunch in the revolving restaurant at the top of the CN tower, where you'll be able to enjoy a three sixty view of our city," said Jonathan as she climbed back into bed to find orange juice, croissants and coffee now laid out on her bedside cabinet.

"That sounds amazing, but won't we be lucky to get a table at such short notice?" she asked, slipping back into her professional role. "Under normal circumstance yes, but Shaun and I have a standing reservation for a table for four on the third Tuesday of every month when we use the occasion to entertain respective clients, and luckily, today happens to be the day," he explained.

"That all sounds terribly organised my love," she replied. It was the first time she'd used the endearment and it had not gone unnoticed.

It was over lunch, surrounded by spectacular views over the city, that Jonathan at last felt comfortable about raising the question of Brad's trunk, wondering what Corinne would like to do about it. Having spent so much time and effort delving into the Meyer family past, his instinct was to go ahead and open it, despite still feeling a little guilty about his father's reluctance, but as Brad was her father, he really felt the decision should be hers.

"We're all having such a lovely holiday that an instinctive part of me is saying you should ask Lewis to dig a deep hole in some quiet corner of your lovely garden and bury it and that Laura and I should move on, because I know that's what she'd want. After all, before your turning up in Little Oreford, neither of us had spared a thought for Brad," she rationalised.

"I know it's nothing to do with me, but my gut feeling is that you should bury it Corinne," agreed Shaun.

"What possible good can come from knowing the secrets which may be lurking in inside, especially as Brad was operating under some cloud that was actually in danger of besmirching the good name of the Meyer practice," he pointed out.

"What do you think Alicia?" Corinne asked.

"The decision has to be down to you and Jonathan, but like Shaun, I can't see the point in whistling up possible spectres from the past to haunt you when there's no pressing need," she said.

"So, we'll leave the tempting red apple right where it is on the tree and bury it in our Garden of Eden shall we?" asked Jonathan. "Yes, I think so," Corinne replied quietly. Now she'd found Jonathan, her desire to find out what had become of her obviously errant father had lost its appeal.

"Then I give you a toast to the future and suggest we celebrate with a trip to Niagara, where the falls should look magnificent at this time of the year," said Shaun. calling over Mark, their favourite waiter, and ordering a bottle of Champagne.

"I know you said you'd need to be back in the office tomorrow, but surely a couple more days off wouldn't really hurt under the circumstances, would it Jonathan," Shaun pleaded.

Corinne and Alicia looked at him expectantly. "It seems like I have no option," he said, laughing.

At some point during their autumn visit to the falls, Lewis did as he'd been bid and buried Brad's trunk four feet deep in a quiet corner of the garden.

Corinne and Alicia spent the next three days happily exploring Toronto before meeting up with Jonathan and Shaun for supper and then on to bed in their host's respective houses. The following weekend they all drove up to the Meyer family lakeside camp and spent a happy couple of days messing about in canoes and with Shaun patiently teaching them to paddle board, but their time together was inexorably drawing to a close and was tinged with a bitter sweetness.

Corinne and Jonathan were now seriously in love, but both recognised that getting properly together was, in reality, going to be impossible.

They had completely separate lives in different time zones and separated by over three thousand miles of ocean.

A long-distance relationship was the only practical option, but they could Skype every couple of days and there was nothing to stop Corinne flying over once a quarter for two or three weeks at a time, but for Alicia, there could be no such option.

"I'm beginning to wish I'd stayed at home so would never have put myself in this miserable situation," she confessed, as they were enjoying a last lunch at what had become their favourite lakeside café bar and were due to fly home the following evening. She'd called home several times, now beginning to wish that Royston would make her feel wanted by saying just how much he was missing her, but no, he was all wrapped up in his world as usual and she got the impression he was actually enjoying the freedom of not having her around, which somehow made her plight that much more awful to bear.

"How does Shaun feel?" Corinne asked, stretching out and giving her friend's hand a supportive squeeze. "He knows I'd never tear my little family apart, for Anthony's sake, so we've both agreed that it's best that when we board that flight tomorrow. then that will be the end of everything," she said, now very close to tears.

"But does it have to be Alicia, because what would prevent you from coming back with me, provided I don't go in the school holidays? We could just say we're hooked on exploring Canada and leave it at that," she suggested, "Do you really think it would work? asked Alicia, her hopes beginning to rise before the doubts set in. "No, that would mean going on living a lie and, despite everything, I don't want to go on doing that," she declared.

It was Shaun who drove them back to the airport for their Air Canada flight as Jonathan had a booked meeting with an important client that he could not avoid. He and Alicia had said their farewells in bed most of that morning, only emerging at lunchtime to join Corinne and Karen for a light lunch, and then leaving her to spend the afternoon packing. He unloaded their cases from his boot and found them a trolly before finally leaving them with a communal hug in the departure hall. "Until next time then," he said smiling, before turning and walking away.

Chapter 9

It had been arranged that Bob would pick them up from Heathrow in his Bentley, now on semi-permanent hire to Royston, who'd long since given up driving himself around his steadily expanding estate agency empire, spending his time far more productively on the phone while on the move.

"So, what's all the 'goss' then?" asked Corinne, once they were safely back on the M4 and heading west.

"Yes, go on Bob, spill the beans," encouraged Alicia, who was now feeling in a much happier mood, having made up her mind on the flight that Shaun must be just a happy memory and that she really would try to rekindle some romantic feelings for her husband.

They'd agreed not to contact one another and Shaun had made no secret of the fact that he would most likely revert to his former arrangement with the two high-flying professional single women, who were married to their careers, but needed a little occasional comforting. Shaun had been brutally honest over this admission and it had helped with Alicia's resolve to try and make a better go of her marriage.

Corinne was also fully in the picture because Jonathan had eventually admitted that the pink silk dressing gown had in fact been worn on the odd occasion by one of Shaun's 'friends.

But in his case, that garment was bound for the bin and when Corinne returned, a blue silk one, to match his own would be laid out on her side of the bed, she'd been promised.

"Let's face it Alicia, those two have got their professional and personal lives pretty much sorted out," said Corinne, after they'd discussed the 'friends' revelation and the monthly luncheon reservation in the revolving restaurant on top of the CN Tower.

It took Bob a good thirty minutes to bring them up to speed with all that had been going on during their absence. "Annie says the inn's been pretty busy and that a spot inspection of the kitchen by health inspectors shortly after you departed all went well according to Andy. "Well, that's a relief, isn't it?" said Alicia. "Yes, but no surprise really because he does run a pretty tight ship when it comes to hygiene and all aspects of health and safety," Corinne replied.

"Have you and Royston been far lately Bob?" asked Alicia, who was used to seeing his Bentley sweeping along their drive to pull up in front of their house several times a week. "I suppose you know all about the firm's latest acquisition," he replied conversationally. "No. not really because Royston only mentioned it while we were away, but I gather we're now moving north into Somerset," she said. "That's right, into Minehead on the coast to be precise." Then the car phone burst into life and Royston's still boyish voice filled the space. "Hi Bob, are the girls safely home?" he asked. "Yes, we are and we've had an amazing time because Jonathan and his mother Karen were really great hosts," Alicia replied. "I expect you'll be tired and want a rest when you get back, but I won't be late home because we've had a bit of a week this week, haven't we Bob?" said Royston. "Yes. you could say that," Bob responded.

Climbing into bed and snuggling up to Royston's, now quite rotund body, was a really weird experience after two weeks of Shaun's lithe and muscular form, but she'd made an effort and put on some of his favourite perfume. She'd fully expected he'd fall asleep in just a couple of minutes as usual, given the exhaustive pace at which his working days were spent, but to her surprise, he suddenly rolled over and wrapped his arms around her. "It might not have seemed like it, but I really have missed you, you know." Suddenly the familiarity of him and all they'd shared over their years, tugged at her heartstrings and, tinged with a sense of guilt, and the need to atone for it, they made love with a vigour that had eluded them for years.

Corinne was quickly submerged in her busy life once more and had easily persuaded Laura and Ben that a desperately needed restaurant conservatory extension should be prioritised ahead of a second B&B acquisition. She and Jonathan Skyped at least four times a week in the privacy of her room and were already making plans about what they should do on her return. "We've Christmas fast approaching and that's actually our busiest time of the year, but then everything falls flat in January, so that's when, realistically, I could next get away for a week or so," she told him.

"Come for New Year, after which we'll fly down to Florida for a couple of weeks and get some sun," he suggested.

She and Alicia had not spoken for several months when her friend text her an invitation to meet for lunch at their usual Italian. Corinne could see the moment she approached her, that all was not well.

"What's the matter?" she asked, her voice full of concern, as soon as she was seated. "I think I'm pregnant," Alicia announced flatly. Corinne sat in silence for a few moments trying to recover from the shock. "Do you think its Royston's or Shaun's?" she enquired.

"How on earth should I know," Alicia replied, suddenly unfolding a neatly placed paper table napkin and blowing her nose. Antonio, the always genial restaurant owner, who'd been idly watching his only guests from behind his plastic flower-decked bar, rolled his eyes. "Have you and Royston made love since your return?" she asked. "Yes, we have, so I'm hoping it's his, but the idea of being pregnant again at forty-two and going though that whole bringing up a baby business is the very last thing I want," she sniffed. "Oh, Alicia I'm so, so sorry." Corinne replied quietly. "It's not your fault, I should just have been more bloody careful," she said, thinking back to that first night of unprotected sex she'd enjoyed with Shaun when high on excitement Champagne and red wine.

"I take it you haven't broken the news to Royston yet," she said.

"No, but I know he'll be over the moon because he's always wanted another child and when it didn't happen, I guess we both just accepted we weren't going to have any more kids," she explained. "But what if you made it clear that it's your body and you simply don't want to go through all that again?" she suggested. "He'd accept it, but I know it would break his heart and honestly, he's a good man and I just couldn't do that to him," she admitted. "But what if the baby looks absolutely nothing like him?" Corinne pointed out. "He might have his doubts, but I'm pretty sure he'd keep them to himself, especially if the baby was a girl," she replied.

"So that's settled then and I volunteer to organise the baby shower!" Corrine announced, in an attempt to lighten their mood.

"That's not funny Corinne, not even coming from you!" Alicia retorted. "No that was right out of order," she apologised. Then a thought struck her. "I guess I'd better not tell Jonathan because he'd never be able to resist telling Shaun and that might really complicate matters," she rationalised. "No don't do that whatever you do," agreed Alicia. "Shaun and I agreed before we left that ours had been strictly a holiday thing and I made it pretty clear that I wouldn't be in touch again and would be more than unhappy if he tried to contact me."

Corinne drove back to Little Oreford deep in thought. She hadn't told Alicia she was planning to fly back out to Toronto just after New Year and then on down to Florida, or that she and Jonathan were now really close and full-on in their long-distance relationship. Alicia had asked after him, but she'd played it all down in the circumstances.

All was quiet in The Oreford Inn on her return and Annie, on reception, had little to report, other than that she had a rather bad headache, so Corinne said she should go home and rest. Annie seemed to be having quite a lot of headaches lately, which wasn't like her, she mused. Then the reception phone rang.

"Oh Corinne. I'm glad it's you," said Laura, a note of agitation in her voice. "Luke brought his new girlfriend home for lunch and she's here for supper and staying over, but I don't like her one bit," her twin confided. She's very outspoken and self-opinionated and not a bit like Judith, who finally gave up on him for showing no interest in having a family. So will you come over for a meal later and give me some moral support?" she pleaded.

"But won't Ben be there?" she asked, playing for time. "No, he's got some meeting to go to, so it's going to be just me and Luke and her, unless you can come," she stressed. Damn, she was really looking forward to Skyping Jonathon later, but now she'd have to email him and postpone until tomorrow.

The evening wasn't that bad, as it turned out, especially as Corinne was mildly interested in the climate change debate, while Laura had no interest in it whatsoever and she didn't think Ben had either. Far better for Luke to have someone in his life who shared his passions, rather than a young woman, who was really more interested in starting a family, she mused as she made her way back to the inn.

But the minute Jonathan's face filled her laptop screen the following evening, she knew all was not well. "What's the matter Jonathan?" she asked. "Pandora's box has been opened!"n came his shock reply. "What on earth do you mean?" she asked, beginning to feel worried. "I mean that before Lewis had time to bury my Great Uncle Frank's trunk, as we'd all agreed he should, mother opened it and read some of the papers," he replied.

"Why on earth should she do that?" asked Corinne in disbelief.

"Because she felt my father was wrong to deny you access and that one day you might have regretted your decision. And, of course, I made it easier for her by purposely cleaning off the mouldy old fastenings in case you should want to look inside" he explained.

"So why didn't she simply keep quiet about what she'd found," Corinne wondered. "She hadn't intended telling me what she'd done, but then when she realised what she'd discovered, she felt she had no alternative but to tell me," he said.

"Oh my God Jonathan, what a shock," she sympathised. "So what could possibly have been among the papers that was so important that it would have been impossible to keep quiet about it?" she asked. There was a long and painful pause. "It turns out, reading between the lines, that Brad badgered and eventually persuaded his father Frank and my grandfather Joe, who were the senior partners in our family firm, to sign over ownership of our now immensely valuable old building in central Toronto to some adventure capital company based in the Costa Rican capital San Jose, as security for some mega deal," he explained.

"But why on earth would they do that and, more importantly, is it really true?" There was another heavy silence. "I can't imagine why they did it, but unfortunately, it is true. As soon as I was told this, I drove to the office and went down into the vault where we keep all our clients' confidential family files and straight to our locked steel box, which I knew from father was where our deeds were stored," he explained. "Our deeds, which father had said were kept sealed and wrapped in a waxed and bulky package and tied with red ribbon, had indeed gone, and in their place, was another document in a large manilla envelope. Inside it, was confirmation that ownership of our building and a neighbouring parcel of real estate, worth together around forty million dollars today, was now held by some organisation called Agrimenta Investments Incorporated of San Jose," he said.

"It appears that we are now in possession of a rent-free annual self-renewing lease expiring ten years from now, after which our entire property will belong to someone else!" he revealed. "Oh my God Jonathon, how terrible. I can see why your poor mother realised this was something she couldn't possibly keep to herself."

Then a thought occurred to her. "So surely, she actually did the right thing by opening the trunk, otherwise it would have been buried and no one would have known of its contents, and you and your family would have got a terrible shock to one day receive a letter from some firm of corporate lawyers requiring you to vacate your own premises," she pointed out.

"But it does seem strange to me that you, and obviously your father, took it on trust from your grandfather that the deeds were in that box and that neither of you ever felt the need to take a look at them, otherwise all this would have come to light years ago," she pointed out. "You're right. I guess it's just one of those things," agreed Jonathan. "So what are you going to do about it?" she asked. "Well, firstly I plan to share all this with Shaun, and then, if it's OK with you, I thought we'd forget Florida after Christmas and head on down to San Jose and see what we can find out," he suggested. "I'm well up for that Jonathan," she said, experiencing counter feelings of both trepidation and excitement.

When they'd finished talking, Jonathan grabbed a larger from the fridge and wandered out onto the patio. It was dusk on a chilly early November evening and getting dark, but he'd been ensconced with his laptop all day and now needed to get some air and to start thinking clearly about just what was to be done.

His mother had gone off to stay with her younger sister for a couple of days to recover from the shock and had felt it best that he enjoyed some space.

If they were going down to San Jose to 'look around,' it seemed only sensible that he should set some prior investigative enquiries in hand, so that they'd at least have one or two leads to follow up, but just how was he to go about that? He mused.

Shaun was luckily free for dinner at a down town restaurant they'd frequented on the odd occasion after work, and pushed the remains of a not particularly exciting starter around his plate while Jonathan explained the situation.

"That's a pig of a problem, but I do have a couple of extremely reliable contacts in Central America and I'll see if they've ever heard of Agrimenta Investments Incorporated of San Jose.

At least it would be a start. Oh! and has Corinne mentioned Alicia lately? he probed. "Funnily enough she did tell me a couple of weeks ago that she and her husband and their son were flying off to the Canary Islands for an early New Year break, but that was about it really."

Shaun wondered if Alicia had deliberately asked Corinne to pass on this news as a silent signal that it really was all over between them, although he didn't pursue it. The truth was that although he'd gone along with her making the point that their's was only a holiday romance, he'd really missed her, and the practical arrangement which he, and formerly Jonathan, had in place when it came to sex, had somehow lost its appeal.

It was a couple of days later that he called Jonathan up at the office to say that surprisingly, and quite unexpectedly, he did have some news. It seemed that Agrimenta Investments was a fund used as a vehicle through which long term loans were handed out to those embarking on large infrastructure and other projects. His contact believed it was a a subsidiary of the Jimarenal Corporation. which had business interests throughout Central and South America. "That's brilliant news Shaun, so it might simply be a case of chasing down the fund administrators and finding out just how they came to be in possession of our family real estate, if indeed they are still in possession of it and have not sold it on to a third party. At least this has given us a starting point. I wonder if your contact, who came up with this gem, has any associates inside investment finance circles in San Jose."

Shaun said he'd find out and they arranged to meet up for lunch in couple of days.

The run up to Christmas was a busy time on both sides of the pond. While Jonathan and the team at Joseph B Meyer were suddenly confronted with a build-up of litigation cases, Corinne and all at The Oreford Inn were busy coping with a rush of festive parties and family celebrations.

Chapter 10

Christmas in Costa Rica commences with the Festival de la Luz in the second week of December when the capital San Jose is festooned in garlands of lights. A huge parade from Passeo Colon, the central avenue, to El Parque de la Democracia takes place early on the second Saturday evening and making his way purposely through the crowd was one Victor Rodrigues and he was not in a good mood. Escaping from this human tide, he hurried up a darkened and narrow side street, a couple of blocks over from the parade, and into a dimly lit bar where all was suddenly quiet, although distant sounds from the grand parade could still be heard. The barman gave him a cursory nod as he pushed aside a beaded curtain and hurried up the stairs to enter a room on the first floor. "You are late." chided a man of bulky proportions, who was sitting around a table with four others.

"Apologies," muttered Victor, shrugging off the reprimand as he took off his smart overcoat to reveal a dark evening suit.

All those in the room were also suited and seemed totally out of place in their shabby surroundings.

They'd all grown up in this neighbourhood and had, in fact, dreamed up their business enterprise in this very room.

While all now occupied smart homes in desirable addresses around or close by the city, meeting back here on the odd occasion when danger threatened was like returning to the womb. They now owned the whole block and didn't really care that the bar, run by a trusted associate, simply jogged along without really making any money.

"So what's this all about Victor?" the big man asked as soon as the latecomer was settled in his seat. The six of them, roughly all in their mid-fifties, never trusted using their mobile phones for transmitting anything other than the most banal of messages because who could tell who might be listening. This golden rule had largely helped to maintain the secrecy of their whole operation. While they deeply distrusted mobiles because one's whereabouts could be compromised, they certainly used tracking technologies when it came to relieving extremely wealthy visitors of their top of the range vehicles.

Victor instinctively leant forward, as if he were in a crowded room and others could be listening, which was ridiculous. but there again, the habits of a lifetime in the shadows were too hard to break. Had he known it, this simple precaution would have been worth it because the room had been bugged and had been so for months by serious crime officers waiting patiently for this targeted group to meet there.

"Word has come down that we should make discrete enquires and report back if we happen to hear that a Canadian businessman named Meyer has turn up, and that applies especially to you Sebby with all your hotel connections."

Sebastian Mora was slightly built and made up for his diminutive stature by being a natural charmer and this was his most deceptive quality as he was by far the most ruthless member of the group.

He was on friendly terms with hotel concierges around the city, who would occasionally pass on information about wealthy guests, which might be useful, particularly if they owned top of the range motors which could be electronically tagged and later liberated.

Ironically his most prolific informant was one George O'Brien, whose father, named after a close relative, was raised in the maritime city of Bristol before going to sea and eventually finding his way to Costa Rica. "I'll make some enquiries," he said, getting to his feet, being anxious to join his friends and not to miss any more of the festive celebrations and signalling that the meeting was over. No one spoke, once they'd left the room and all went their separate ways.

Senior Serious Crime Intelligence Officer Alex Gonzales was in a particularly good mood that following Monday morning, despite still having a slightly sore head from the weekend's festive celebrations. It had become a tradition for him and his close-knit serious crime squad colleagues to make the Festival de la Luz the occasion for their annual Christmas party and he was not the only one with a lingering hangover.

Alex was in a good mood because, after months of surveillance, they now had the names Sebastian and Meyer to go on, with Sebastian being the most important because they now knew he'd be making the rounds of his hotel contacts for news of an arriving guest called Meyer, who was clearly of particular importance to this illusive organisation.

"So, all we have to do now is to make discreet enquiries around all the hotels concerning an arriving guest called Meyer and then put a tail on him, and equally importantly, see if we can identify this Sebastian as he makes his rounds and put a tail on him," Alex told his small team at a briefing later that morning.

Listening intently, was Cristina Morales, the latest recruit and only woman on the team.

She had already earned the grudging respect of her seven male colleagues for being worth her weight in pure gold. Chrissie, as they all called her, was highly ambitious and had, as they later discovered, few scruples when it came to pursuing her 'prey' as she called them. If she judged going to bed was going to be the best way to extract some valuable information, then that's exactly what she did. She'd joined the squad some nine months earlier and had been the hot topic of conversation among her male colleagues in her earlier days. She'd socialise with them in quiet times, but kept a lid on her private life, so they had no idea where she went or what she did after hours. She seemed to show little interest in men, except in the line of duty, but on the other hand they all found it difficult to believe she was gay. In the end they gave up speculating and just accepted that Chrissie was Chrissie and that was the end of it.

Chapter 11

Corinne's London-Toronto flight departed Heathrow at 9am on a Saturday morning. She'd stayed overnight at a chain hotel, but had not slept much because of the sheer anticipation of being with Jonathan again and all that might lay ahead.

'I'll get some rest on the flight,' she thought, having treated herself to business class, but again sleep had eluded her.

He was there to meet her, wearing a woollen hat and heavy overcoat because it was freezing outside the terminal.

It was like hugging a bear, she thought, as their lips met in a hungry kiss, before they hurried out to his car.

They were in his big bed within the hour because neither of them wanted to wait a moment longer and after their hurried love-making she fell into a deep sleep fuelled by a heady mix of passion and exhaustion.

It was late afternoon when she awoke and slipped naked out of bed and into a chunky white robe, which he'd thoughtfully laid out alongside the promised blue silk number. She smiled, remembering the cherry pink gown he'd fetched from his wardrobe after their first night in bed together.

Walking to the large picture window, she slowly drew back the heavy curtains and revealed a hushed white world. There was the sharp sound of wood being chopped nearby. 'I wonder if that's Lewis at work,' she thought.

She dressed and went down to find Jonathan in his study on his laptop with Toronto to San Jose flight information up on his screen.

It was his cosy, manly, intimate space, dominated by the large Chesterfield on which they had enjoyed a nightcap on their first night. "That was well timed," he said, reaching up, without turning, to connect with the hand she'd placed on his shoulder.

"We can catch a flight just before 9am and be in San Jose around four in the afternoon. We'll be in the air for just over five hours, but they're two hours ahead of us," he said.

"I bet it's going to be a lot warmer than here," she replied.

"It's 17 degrees and sunny at the moment, but pretty humid, I imagine," he said after making a rapid search on the keys.

"Shaun's invited us over for supper. He's been doing quite a bit of research into Agrimenta Investments Incorporated via his contacts in Central America and has more info to give us," said Jonathan. "That's great," Corinne replied, but in that moment, she began feeling that it wasn't really that great at all and she just wished they were going for a relaxing holiday. She already knew what her father looked like and a little of his past history and now she had Jonathan, did she really want to know what had become of him? The Oreford had enjoyed its busiest ever Christmas and, what with that, and Laura and Ben being totally wrapped up in all their expansion plans, she was quite mentally and physically tired. All she really wanted to do was to chill out beside some hotel pool with a good book for a couple of weeks and perhaps do a little sightseeing. "There you both are," said Jonathan's mother, suddenly appearing in the doorway. They hugged and she asked how the flight had been before announcing that her cab would be arriving shortly. "Oh, I do hope I'm not driving you out of your own home," said Corinne.

"No dear. My younger sister and I are following in your footsteps and are off on a fly cruise around the Caribbean to soak up some sun, so perhaps we'll bump into you," she replied. "No mother, Costa Rica is in Central America and not the Caribbean," he chided her gently.

Supper at Shaun's was a low-key, help yourself cold buffet affair because Lewis and Lois were having a night off, but that suited Corinne who was still feeling tired and wasn't really in the mood for socialising. Glass of wine in hand, she'd wandered over to the window, overlooking the patio and pool, and was instantly remembering them all fooling around, naked in the water.

What a lot had happened since then, she thought.

It had not been long before Shaun was asking after Alicia, and she'd immediately felt guilty at not being able to share her news with him, or even Jonathan. "Oh she, Royston and their son Anthony are soaking up some winter sun in the Canary Islands at the moment," she said, as if to subtly reinforce that it really was over between them.

"Santa Cruz de Tenerife is four hours ahead of Toronto and at that moment, Alicia and Royston were lying in bed together.

He was on his side and gently caressing her small swelling. Every now and again his fingers would stray into her forest, sending a mildly urgent tingling sensation around her groin. Royston, as she'd so rightly anticipated, had been over the moon about their baby and her pregnancy had rekindled the embers of their relationship. Even so, she couldn't help thinking about

Shaun now and again, but kept pushing any thoughts that the baby might be his to the back of her mind. When supper was over, Shaun revealed he'd now found an address for Agrimenta Investments, which strangely seemed to be in a complex of municipal or state administration buildings.

It turned out that Shaun's close contact in Panama City had a colleague in San Jose, called Manny, who would be willing to assist and act as their interpreter and he'd supplied a telephone number. "That's an incredible bit of luck Shaun. Having a local on side, so we won't be hampered by the language barrier is a real bonus," said Jonathan.

"It must be really great having such a close friend as Shaun. I've never managed to be really close to anyone until you came into my life, which is rather sad don't you think?" she said as they sat together in his den enjoying a nightcap. They'd just been online and booked their early morning flights for the day after tomorrow and chosen an upmarket chain hotel set in a coffee plantation with a pool and all the other luxury necessities for having a chill out time."You're close to your sister and Ben and, of course, your amazingly indefatigable mum," he pointed out. "Yes, but that's family and they're different to a close friend and, besides that, I didn't know

I had any of them until a few years ago, remember," she reminded him. "But what about Alicia?" he persisted gently. "Surely she's your confidant, just like Shaun is mine." Again, she came close to telling him that her friend was pregnant, but again, she drew back, feeling guilty for doing so because if she couldn't trust Jonathan to keep her secret then just who could she trust? "Yes, Alicia is my only close friend, but there's an aloofness to her. It's as if there's a whole lot going on in her head that she doesn't want to share with me," she explained. Jonathan thought about this for a few moments, toying with his glass of single malt whisky as he did so.

"I guess we all have some things going on deep inside that we're often reluctant to talk about or don't quite know how to," he admitted.

Chapter 12

Manuel Varga, known as Manny to his close associates, certainly had a lot going on in his head that he had no intention of sharing with anyone and it mostly concerned his international stock market activities. He often sailed close to the wind in his dealings, which was ironic seeing that international shipping was his area of expertise, but not that close because being too close for comfort was not a space he wanted to occupy. He rather saw himself as a small fry nibbling the mites off the back of the bigger fish swimming around in his pond, but he was, he had to admit, rather good at it and had become quite wealthy in the process. Manny's closest associate was based in Panama City and it was he who had asked if he could assist one Jonathan Meyer, who was due to fly in shortly from Toronto, and would be giving him a call. Juan Santa Maria Airport is located in the city of Alajuela, some twelve miles west of down town San Jose. They touched down in late afternoon and were in their master suite at the Hotel Alhambra within the hour. A complimentary bottle of sparkling wine lay in its ice bucket together with two flutes, a bowl of exotic fruit and a compliments card from the General Manager. It was an extra provided for all those booking the most expensive suites, but still made Corinne feel special. They popped the cork and strolled out onto the balcony two relax in two expensive wicker loungers. "I could get really used to this Jonathan," she said. "Come off it. I bet you'd be bored in ten minutes," he said.

"You're probably right," she admitted, thinking of the buzz she got from running The Oreford Inn.

Over dinner in the hotel's lavish restaurant, they decided on a plan of action. "I think we should make our enquiries first and see where that takes us and then we should reward ourselves by having a holiday, because I don't think I'm going to be able to relax properly beforehand," Corinne told him. "Then that's what we'll do and I'll call this Manny straight after breakfast," Jonathan promised.

Not far away across the city, Senior Serious Crime Officer Alex Gonzalez was about to leave his office when word came through from airport passport control that one Canadian national, Jonathan Andrew Meyer, had entered the country accompanied by a British national, a Miss Corinne Potter. The chances were that they'd taken a taxi to an hotel where their passport details would have been logged on registration, he reasoned, so he'd have a call round actioned immediately. By the time he'd got back into the office, the following morning, it had been established that the two were staying at the Hotel Alhambra and arrangements were quickly made to have their suite bugged at soon as it became possible later that day.

"If our target organisation has asked their associates to be on the look-out and to report back if they hear the name Meyer, might it be reasonable to assume that this person is perceived as being some form of threat to them?" Alex suggested at a team briefing, called as soon as everyone was in. "And that being the case, might it also be reasonable to assume that this pair might be willing to cooperate with our investigations?" he argued. No one saw the need to question his assumptions, so the room remained silent, apart from the eratic flow from the air con system that was probably almost as old as their 'new' building.

"OK so how do we proceed from here on in?" he questioned, putting them all suddenly on the spot. First to respond was the largely overweight Pascual, whose French grandparents had pitched up on the Caribbean coast of Costa Rica to grow bananas around the port of Moin, now the epicentre of a huge banana growing and export operation. Pascual might have been large, but he was all muscle, quick witted and could move at the speed of a polar bear if circumstances demanded, which was a great advantage as it had often caught his adversaries completely off their guard. "Our first step must be to put an immediate two man watch on the Alhambra reception and instruct the team there to give us a nod just as soon as someone comes sniffing around asking after Meyer," he suggested. "We'll need one to tail this Sebastian, if he shows up, and the other to follow Meyer and the woman. It's critical we get to them before the other side do and seeing they only checked in yesterday afternoon, I think we can assume we're already one step ahead on this one." he reasoned. "OK off you go then Pascual and Frankie," Alex instructed. The big man got slowly to his feet, supressing a broad smile as he did so. It was the perfect assignment. A legitimate opportunity for him and his usual side-kick to spend hours relaxing in armchairs in the delicious air-conditioned coolness of The Alhambra's extensive tile floored foyer, catching up on the news in all the complimentary newspapers and glossy magazine. "Oh! and Pascual. Don't forget these," Alex said handing over copies of Jonathan and Corinne's passport photos which had been emailed over by the hotel manager. Chrissy Morales had assumed she was being assigned to watch out for this Sebastian, from something her boss had said earlier, but there again wating around in a hotel lobby for hours was not really her scene so she'd said nothing.

Corinne slipped out of bed around 6am, disturbed by a cacophony of bird song and out onto the balcony overlooking the pool and the plantation. The sky was clear blue, apart from a skein of jet trails and her spirits rose at the thought that it was below freezing in Toronto and damp and cold back in Little Oreford. They'd not had any snow in their part of North Devon for some years now, so surely yet another worrying sign of global warming, as her nephew Luke would say. But January and February were still her least favourite months and she couldn't think why in the past she'd not taken a break and flown off to some warmer, if not exotic, part of the world, like Alicia and Royston. But she was making up for it now and in the future she and Jonathan would go off exploring, may be to Australia and New Zealand. But before they could truly relax now, there was this tedious business of trying to find out who held the lease to his family real estate and that cast a small shadow over her mood. Brushing it off, she slipped back into their huge bed intent on rousing Jonathan, but not only from sleep!

It was 9.45am by the time they finally descended the curving flight of wide marble stairs with its ornate metal balustrade and into the plant filled conservatory where breakfast was being served.

Pascual and Frankie had already taken up their strategically chosen positions in the hotel foyer where, between them, they could cover the long reception desk and the entrance lobby.

Over breakfast, Jonathan, called Manual Varga only to hear a cultured Spanish voice saying he was not available at this time. Speaking slowly, although he was sure Sen Varga spoke excellent English, he left a short explanatory message asking him to get in touch. "Seeing we can't do any more than that at the moment, which is a bit frustrating, we might as well spend the day seeing what San Jose has to offer the tourist until he contacts us," suggested Jonathan.

They spent a happy time taking a walking tour and spending hours, including lunch, in the city's bustling Central Market, which, according to their guide book, opened in 1880, was one of the oldest landmarks in the country.

It was late afternoon when they eventually got back to their now spotlessly serviced room and Sen Manual Varga called. He did, of course, speak excellent English and sounded both courteous and charming with the self-assured air of a confidant so Jonathan quickly explained the business reason for their being in San Jose. "It all sounds quite intriguing, so I'll drop by for coffee tomorrow morning and meet you in the lobby say around 11am?" he suggested. "I think Shaun might have found just the right man to help us," said Jonathan, putting down his mobile on his bedside table, close to the tiny bug now cleverly concealed there!

Chapter 13

Pascual had spent a fruitless day in the hotel foyer having sent Frankie off to follow the Meyers on their sightseeing tour around town as soon as they were spotted leaving the lobby. No one had turned up enquiring after the Meyers, he told Frankie, who'd wandered back into the foyer and casually taken a seat next to him, but then his mobile rang and there was a brief conversation.

"The boss wants me back in the office pronto, but you're to remain here, say until around ten just in case this Sebastian shows up." Frankie rolled his eyes. He'd long ago resigned himself to the fact that the working hours directive rule book had been tossed into the wastepaper basket in their section. Still, it was as well he was a loner without much else to do, he consoled himself.

Back in the office, Alex now in possession of a full transcript of the conversation between Jonathan Meyer and Sen Manuel Varga, read it out to his team after Pascual had returned and had settled his bulk against a grubby wall with his arms folded. "I think this is good news for us," he declared, once they'd all had a few moments to consider this new intelligence. "I don't think Sen Meyer and his girlfriend have a clue as to what they are about to walk blindly into with the assistance of this Sen Varga, who we need to check out soonest," he said, looking across at Chrissie Morales. "I'm on it, boss," she responded. "If you can dig up some background overnight, it might be advantageous as I think I'm going to invite myself along to this meeting at The Alhambra, tomorrow," said Alex.

Frankie must have closed his eyes for just a few moments because he failed to spot Sebastian Mora slip into the hotel carrying a special delivery parcel for one Sen Meyer. There was nothing in the small parcel, but it gave him a legitimate cover for his tedious day long round of hotel enquiries which had suddenly hit the jackpot. Sebbie, for that was his nickname, should have been pleased, but cursed himself for having decided to keep San Jose's more exclusive crop of hotels, to last. He'd reasoned that this Sen Meyer would probably have wanted somewhere less conspicuous to stay, but he'd been wrong. Yet it was a blessing in disguise because had he appeared that morning, it was almost certain he'd have been spotted and would now have become the hunted rather than the hunter. He'd also been lucky because the hotel's late evening receptionist was a temporary, who'd not been instructed to alert Frankie should anyone appear asking for a Sen Meyer.

Alex had decided that Chrissie should accompany him to The Alhambra the following morning because Sen Meyer's companion was an attractive woman and his instincts told him this would make his intended intervention less threatening.

"I got lucky checking out Manual Varga because he carries on his international stock market dealings very much in the open," she told him soon after they driven away from the office.

"He appears to be an important player in several trade associations, so I think there's absolutely nothing devious in his agreement to assist Sen Meyer other than doing a favour for his colleague in Panama City."

They quickly spotted Pascual settled in his usual leather chair and, casually walking over, they took the empty seats opposite.

"The Meyers met Sen Varga at the tourist information desk a couple of minutes ago and they've all gone out to the café bar beside the pool," he said quietly, without looking up.

Alex and Chrissie stepped out onto the raised patio above the pool area, looking across at the café bar with its cluster of smart wicker chairs under sun umbrellas and quickly spotted the three. Luckily, a nearby table was free, so they made their way towards it, ordering soft drinks from the waiter, who swiftly intercepted them. From their vantage point, they could almost hear their conversation, but gave up trying after a couple of minutes and were distracted by the arrival of their drinks. Sen Varga listened intently as Jonathan again carefully laid out all the reasons for their visit and when he'd finished, sat pondering it all for a few moments. "I'm sorry Sen Meyer, I've had some time overnight to think about all of this and, on reflexion, I think it's all a little too rich for me. I have a certain position of respect in this town and I'm not sure it would benefit from becoming involved in your enquiries." He paused as if he was carefully choosing his words. "It's not for me to say, Sen Meyer, but I would advise you to enjoy your holiday and go home because if things are, as you say they are, then I am sure you would have a good case for challenging this loss of ownerships in your courts." He got slowly to his feet and so did Jonathan, who thanked him for sparing the time to see them and they shook hands. "Good Luck, Sen Meyer, whatever you decide to do," he said smiling at Corinne before turning and walking away. "So that's that then," said Jonathan sitting down again with a sigh "You mean we should follow his advice?" Corinne asked hopefully.

"No, it means that our quest just got a whole lot harder." Before she could respond, she was suddenly aware of a man in his early forties and an extremely attractive woman, probably in her mid-twenties, walking purposely towards them. Jonathan had his back to them, but following her gaze and alerted by the puzzled look on her face, swung around in his chair.

"Sen Meyer. Do you mind if we join you for a few moments?"

His English was good, spoken in a light Spanish accent, but not in the same league as Manuel Varga. Taken completely by surprise, he waved them into the two vacant chairs.

Alex produced his identity card from where he'd placed it for convenience in the breast pocket of his lightweight regulation blue jacket. "My associate and I are from the Department for the Investigation of Serious Crime, here in San Jose, and have been advised that your visit to Costa Rica is not purely for a holiday."

He could see the shocked look of surprise on both their faces.

"Perhaps you might explain the other reason for your visit?"

Could this be really happening? Jonathan asked himself, taking the policeman's identity card and making a play of examining it while scrambling to gather his thoughts. Corinne, her heart beginning to race, just smiled weakly at the woman beside him.

"We're here for a holiday and to see what we can find out about a family real estate matter back home in Toronto, but I hardly feel it's something for you to concern yourselves about," he replied. "That may be so Sen Meyer, but perhaps you could help by telling us about this family matter."

Needing no further bidding, Jonathan repeated the whole story again, while Corinne sat quietly finding it difficult to believe all this was really happening.

When he'd finally finished, an uncomfortable silence filled the void between them, broken by the splash of someone diving into the nearby pool. "Thank you for that, so now we will explain the situation from our position, which I think will make quite clear to you the reason for our intervention. For several years now, and working in cooperation with other serious crime agencies throughout Central and South America and the Caribbean, we have been trying to penetrate a shady international operation.

Their outwardly legitimate and highly respected persona within government circles is the Jimarenal Corporation. But we know there is also a dark side to their dealings," he revealed, pausing for effect. "This hidden portfolio, I think that is the word you might use, includes money laundering from various narcotics farming enterprises, right across the region and other forms of corruption when it comes to the awarding of government and private civil engineering contracts here in Latin America and in Southern Europe," he revealed.

Jonathan glanced across at Corinne as they both struggled to come to terms with the frightening spider's web of corruption they had so unwittingly wandered in to. No wonder Sen Varga had been reluctant to become involved!

"But surely if you actually know who these people are, and it sounds like a sizeable organisation, then it can't be that difficult to break into their operations," said Jonathan, a note of incredulity in his voice.

Alex took a moment to sip his mango juice, which the ever attentive Chrissie, had carried over to their table for him.

"Believe me, we have spent a considerable amount of our time and resources on this investigation Sen Meyer. But these people are protected by those in high places, who would all have a substantial amount to lose if we busted the Jimarenal Corporation and its subsidiary company, Agrimenta Investments."

Jonathan and Corinne looked at one another, both realising in an instant, that this was the company that might be in possession of his deeds, so no wonder they could be in trouble!

There was another splash in the pool, which only served to heighten their sense of complete unreality as they listened intently to how the serious crime agency had got its first real break some six months earlier.

"This was when we became aware of a highly secretive sub group, operating within the business community here in San Jose," explained Alex. "It was from them we learned, through covert surveillance, that word had come down to keep a watch out for a Canadian called Meyer, who was expected to arrive in San Jose shortly and to report back when they'd found out where he was staying. To that end, one member of the group was assigned to make casual enquiries at every hotel in the city, so we immediately instructed airport immigration officers to alert us the minute you had arrived and had presented your passports for registration," he explained. "So before you came down to breakfast yesterday morning, two members of my team were already keeping watch in the hotel reception area," he revealed.

"This was in case the suspect, who we now know to be one Sebastian Morro, turned up enquiring about you. Had he done so the receptionists would have alerted us. While one kept watch here all day, the other followed you on your tourist round just to make sure you were not intercepted," he revealed.

"That brings us more or less up to date Sen Meyer, so I hope you can now see why we are seriously concerned for your safety," said Alex. "I think that now goes without saying Sen Gonzales, although I can't imagine why my Grandfather should have signed over the deeds of our Toronto property to anyone over thirty years ago. But he obviously did so and they appear to have ended up in the hands of Agrimenta Investments, who have somehow been alerted to our coming here in search of them." Then Corinne had a worrying thought.

"I know you said you'd been keeping a watch out for this Sebastian, but could it be you've missed him and these people already know we are here?" Alex hesitated for a moment.

"I have no wish to alarm you, but yes that is possibility," he conceded. "So, what would you advise us do Sen Gonzales?" asked Jonathan. Alex paused as he considered the question.

"From a purely selfish point of view, we would have

followed you around until these people made contact and maybe given us some fresh leads," he told them. "But, as I hope you can now see, we are not as irresponsible as that, so my advice would be to book your flights home as soon as you can and forget all about this claim on your real estate no matter how valuable it might be."

Now something else occurred to Corinne. "How did you realise we're just a couple of law-abiding people and not part of this money laundering set-up?" she asked. "Let's just say we assumed they see you as some kind of threat to their operations and we reasoned that, if that was the case, then you would be more likely to cooperate with us. So, do you have any other questions?" he asked, "Yes, I do," replied Jonathan. "As you admitted, these people may already know we're here, so are you able to offer us protection until we fly out of here, hopefully tomorrow?" he asked. "Yes, that will be arranged and as an extra precaution we have a small gift for you both," he said looking at Chrissie, who, reaching down, retrieved the leather shoulder bag resting against the leg of her chair.

Opening it, she produced two wrist watches and placed them on the table in front of her. They looked the inexpensive every day sort that a couple might pick up as an impulse buy at any airport duty free store. They stared at them wondering what on earth this was all about. "They may look innocent and certainly not worth anyone trying to steal, but they contain tracking devices and as long as you are wearing them, we are going to know exactly where you are, here in Costa Rica," he explained.

"So, I think that more or less concludes our business unless you have any further questions."

Neither Jonathan nor Corinne replied, now feeling completely overwhelmed by all they'd been told over the past twenty minutes. "Good, then one of my team will remain here in the hotel and follow you out to the airport and all will be fine," he reassured them.

With that, Alex and Chrissie got to their feet and walked away leaving the two of them sitting there in a complete daze.

"I'll go and get my ipad from the room and hopefully we'll be able to fly out of here later today, or sometime tomorrow," said Jonathan, breaking the spell of fear the two visitors had cast over them. "Are you sure you don't need me to come with you?" asked Corinne, already feeling they were in some imminent danger. "No. I'm sure I'll be all right. Why don't you order us some more coffee?" he suggested. "To be honest, I don't think I feel like eating or drinking anything," she replied, sensing some invisible knot tightening in her stomach.

To their huge relief, there was a flight, via Denver, departing at 7pm with seats available so Jonathan booked two in business class because the way he was feeling right now, there was no way he wanted them flying home economy.

"I don't want to sound dramatic, but why don't we go to our room, pack our bags and leave straight away because, to tell you the truth, I think I'd feel a whole lot safer spending the rest of the day in the airport departure lounge, surrounded by lots of people, rather than hanging around here a moment longer than we need to," he suggested.

Pascual, back on watch in an armchair from where he had a clear view of the long reception counter plus the stairs and bank of lifts, was now on full alert having just spoken briefly to Alex and Chrissie before they left. Not long afterwards, he spotted Jonathan hurrying in from the pool area and crossing to the lifts. He watched passively as he reappeared carrying his ipad and disappeared out onto the patio.

'I bet they're booking flights back home, which is what I would do in their situation,' he thought. Then, as if in confirmation of his speculation, they both re appeared and then disappeared into a lift. 'My guess is that when they come down again, they'll be carrying their cases, checking out and heading for the airport, so I'd better be ready to get my arse in gear and follow them,' he told himself.

The couple emerged on cue some thirty minutes later and as they did so, he got up and made his way slowly outside to his motor which, with the hotel's permission, was already parked just behind the no waiting area reserved for cabs delivering and picking up departing guests.

He waited and watched, wondering why they were taking so long to come out, but then they did so with one of the liveried doormen carrying their cases and loading them into the copious boot of a black limousine which had suddenly appeared in front of him. 'Time to go I think,' Pascual told himself as he drove out of the hotel grounds and slotted expertly into the midday flow of traffic just one car back from the 'limo.'

Jonathan and Corinne sat in silence in the brown leather back seats holding hands, but locked in their own thoughts and after a few minutes they noticed the first of a series of comforting Aeroporto signs.

Following behind on a road he'd travelled many times, Pascual began thinking how he might spend the rest of his day which he'd been given off following the long hours of duty he'd put in yesterday. The limo was moving steadily ahead keeping up with the speed of the traffic.

The vehicle was still doing so as they approached the airport boundary with its familiar lines of ancillary buildings and glimpses of parked up jetliners, but then suddenly it had disappeared!

With a squeal of tyres, the big vehicle had suddenly swerved violently to its left, throwing Jonathan and Corinne into a heap despite, their restraining seat belts, before accelerating at great speed along a paved service road for over one hundred yards and screeching to a halt. Before they knew quite what was happening, two big men had climbed into the car, one beside Corinne and the other in the front passenger seat and the vehicle sped off again. "What the hell's going on?" yelled Jonathan suddenly regaining his wits. "Be calm Sen Meyer because I can assure you that no one has any intention of harming either you or Miss Potter," said the 'heavy' in front, who'd turned to face them. "I am called Georges and I have been sent to collect you."

His voice was surprisingly cultured and reassuring, despite its strong Spanish accent.

"You will be flying home, but not quite yet as we are taking you on a small excursion," he said as the limousine pulled up beside a twin prop aircraft parked up with its door open and steps down.

Protest was useless, they could both see that, and there was no point in yelling out because they were on a remote area far from the main terminal building. Hearts thumping and without further protest they were escorted out of the car and towards the steps of the twelve-seater aircraft. As they did so, Jonathan glanced back to see their cases being hefted out of the boot and into a cargo bay at the rear.

Then the most surprising thing happened.

"Would one of you care to take the seat next to the pilot because we'll be flying at no more than twelve thousand feet and the views along the Pacific coast are superb?" Both shook their heads in unison being totally confused by the courteousness of the offer. "That's OK then, but I'll ask you to kindly remove those tracker toys you were given earlier."

They'd both completely forgotten about the watches, but meekly took them off and handed them over because what else could they do? Georges dropped them to the ground and crushed them under the heel of a black and highly polished boot before following them up the steps.

The other man, who'd loaded their luggage and was yet to speak, closed the door behind them before making for the seat beside the pilot.

Jonathan and Corinne chose to sit beside one another, separated by the central aisle, while Georges, who was clearly in charge, sat a couple of rows behind them.

The white shirt-shirted pilot, wearing headphones attached to a wire mic, spoke in rapid Spanish to the control tower while glancing around to check they were all in position, before the twin engines roared into life and the aircraft taxied forward. Quickly airborne, they climbed steeply in the now sunny early afternoon before banking to the west and levelling out as they headed for the Pacific coast.

Why were they being treated more like guests than a couple considered to be a threat to the shadowy organisation that had just gone to a considerable amount of trouble to abduct them? It simply didn't make any sense, thought Jonathan, reaching across and taking Corinne's hand.

Chapter 14
Then

Brad Meyer was already wishing he'd delayed his departure for a few more days even as his taxi sped away from Bristol's smart Star Hotel, through quiet early morning streets and out into the country en-route for Bristol Airport.

He'd just spent probably the most enjoyable twenty-four hours of his life with a beautiful young woman and had fallen madly in love with her. He'd hired her services to give him a guided tour around the historic maritime city on the western seaboard of the UK before flying back home to Toronto via Amsterdam.

Brad was an attractive and highly motivated young man with two fatal flaws, firstly, a rogue streak for ignoring all the rules, if he felt he could get away with it and make a profit into the bargain, and secondly, the ability to rationalize what he had done as actually doing no harm. That was how he'd come to establish his fledgling international investment consultancy while choosing to ignore all the regulatory procedures put in place by the federal government to discourage rogue trading. The business always came first, which was why all his previous relationships had been short-lived.

He'd come to the conclusion he was not really bothered whether he was in a relationship or not, but now he'd met a girl who'd totally excited and captivated him. Her name was Charlie Potter, a final year student at Bristol University, who was highly attractive, very bright and extremely funny. They'd met in the hotel foyer around ten am and had spent the whole day and the night together.

He'd actually got to the point of cancelling his flights home and staying on for a few more days with her until his business instincts finally got the better of him.

But she'd readily agreed to fly out and join him in Toronto just as soon as she'd received an air ticket from him and that was one of the things he loved best about Charlie, namely her completely free spirit.

It was early evening when his KLM flight touched down at Toronto's Lester B Pearson International Airport and he cleared passport control and customs and took a cab back to his down town penthouse pad. It was his only luxury, but one he could not quite justify given the roller coaster ride of his investment portfolio, but still, he could not wait to share it with Charlie.

The green answerphone message light on the end of his central aisle breakfast bar was blinking.

Could that be her calling up already to see if he was home safely? But no, it was one of his key investors seeking an urgent meeting and he did not sound a happy man.

Fighting an overwhelming desire to sleep, he called Harry Jacobs back. The man was clearly in a highly nervous state and demanding they meet up straight away because 'no' this business could not wait until the morning. Reluctantly, he agreed to meet him in their usual place, a quiet bar just a few blocks away. At least the exercise might wake him up, he thought. Entering the bar, he spotted Harry sitting in an alcove and nursing a whisky to calm his nerves. Ordering a strong coffee, he took the seat opposite. "So what's this all about and why is it so important that it could not possibly wait until the morning?" he asked. "I've just flown in from Europe, my head's aching and all I want to do is to sleep," he explained. "You're what it's all about. Yes, you and your sure-fire investment advice. OK you've been spot on so far, but this time you've got it horribly wrong and now I'm in a really serious bind," he admitted. "What do you mean Harry?" Brad asked. "I mean the hot tip you gave me to invest in that mining consortium, poised to announce a major new bauxite deposit in Central America, which would send their share value sky high, turns out to have been a scam and I've lost a small fortune," he admitted.

"Look Harry, I only offer advice and whether or not you choose to accept it is entirely down to you," Brad countered, realising he'd taken his eye off the ball over the past couple of days, not to have been alerted to this worrying development.

He'd given this 'hot tip' to several other of his major investors and no doubt they too would soon be howling for his blood!

"Look Harry, I've always stressed to you and my other clients not to stake more than you can afford to lose so how much are you in for?"

This piece of advice was one of his mechanisms for rationalising that what he was doing, although it was still totally illegal.

"Two million US dollars," replied his friend, downing the last of his malt whiskey and signalling the barman to bring him another.

"Christ that was a bit rich for you, wasn't it?" Brad replied.

"Yes, but that's not the worst of it because it wasn't my money!" he confessed. "Who the hell's was it then?" asked Brad, beginning to have a horrible feeling he was not going to like the answer. "It belonged to a group of

Central American investors, who I have a feeling were using it as a drug money laundering exercise, and now they want their cash back!" he admitted.

"Shit Harry you must have been completely mad to have gone anywhere near them, even if you'd had the slightest suspicion as to what they were up to." Brad countered.

"I know, I know, but I guess I just got greedy because I'd been using them to investment fund all your earlier tips and earning a huge commission, which I also reinvested on my own account," he admitted. "So how on earth are you going to sort this out?" asked Brad.

Harry paused, having taken another slug of whisky which was at last beginning to dull his anxiety. "No. You've got me into this mess, so how are we going to sort this out, because if I go down, then as sure as damn it, I'm going to take you with me," he threatened. "And just how will you do that?" Brad asked quietly, now feeling stone cold sober, as if lack of sleep had been the intoxication. "Firstly, I'll tell these people that I was only the messenger boy and that you're the one they should be chasing for their money. And secondly," he said, pausing for effect. "I'll spread the word around town that your questionable investment advice has been causing hardship and that you're a family member of the highly respected business lawyers Joseph B Meyer and think what that will do for their cherished reputation!"

At that point, Brad could so easily have reached across, grabbed Harry by his jacket lapels and warned him off, but thought better of it because he was weak in both senses of the word and violence was not going to help. "OK Harry you go home now and keep your head down and say nothing about all this to anyone until I've had time to figure something out," he instructed. The look of relief on his investor's face was palpable. " I'll do just that," he promised.

But Brad knew he could not be trusted and that was the worst of it. Back home and now fuelled by a fear fed adrenalin, he made himself another black coffee and sat down to think. But by 3am he'd still failed to come anywhere near working out a plan and mercifully, exhaustion finally took its toll and he fell asleep on his sofa.

Waking around 10am and feeling as if he was recovering from some massive hangover, Brad staggered into the bathroom to take a shower and then decided he need to eat something.

But a few minutes after emerging into his spacious kitchen and breakfast bar area, he heard his answerphone kick in and a cultured Spanish voice speaking excellent English, was asking for him. Brad hesitated, wondering whether or not to pick up the phone. The sensible thing to do might have been to hear what this caller had to say and to respond later, but acting on instinct he picked up the receiver "Brad Meyer speaking," he said hesitantly. "Ah Sen Meyer. You don't know me, but my associates and I know all about you and your family's reputation there in Toronto through your client investor Harry Jacobs."

So Harry had not kept his mouth shut and blown away any bargaining position he might have adopted.

"I'm not sure I know what you're talking about and I certainly don't know who you are," replied Brad, stalling for time.

"Come now Sen Meyer, you know perfectly well what I am talking about and you don't need to know my name, other than that I represent investors whom you have misled and now want to be compensated." A small silence filled the long distance between them.

Brad knew there was no use in pointing out that he only offered advice. Now they knew he was closely linked to a respected Toronto legal firm perceived to be wealthy, then there was no way they were going to be diverted from getting their money back. "So just how much do you believe you are out of pocket?" he asked tentatively.

There was a pause. "I'd say we'd settle for six million US dollars." Brad's heart began thumping.
"But I understood it was two million," he countered.
"Then sadly you are mistaken San Meyer. But listen, we are all reasonable men of the world and up until now your investment advice has been sound, so I am sure we can reach an agreement acceptable to all concerned. Let's say I call you again around this time a week today." Then before Brad had chance to even consider a reply, the line went dead.

Harry was a bloody fool, who'd sold him down the river to save his own skin, so how the hell was he going to extricate himself from this mess and come up with circa six million dollars? He was in no doubt that if he failed to find a solution, there would be retribution both for him and the firm. He knew full well, that any slur on Joseph B Meyer's spotless reputation would break his father's heart and most probably ruin the family firm and all that he and his Uncle Joe had worked for over most of their lives. He'd never really bonded with his father, because of his wild streak, except when sharing the odd fishing trip up at the family's lakeside camp, but there was no way he'd see him upset.

The answerphone interrupted his thoughts and Charlie's voice filled the void. "Hi Brad I've just called to see if you got home OK, but no rush to call me back." He could hear the excitement in her voice.

"I know we've only had a few precious hours together, but I think I love you," she said before putting the receiver down.

"Oh my God. What a bloody nightmare!" he said aloud, now knowing he wouldn't be sending Charlie an airline ticket until he'd found a way of sorting out this goddamn awful mess.

But there just had to be a solution and Brad spent most of the day trying to figure it out. His answerphone kicked in four or five times with other worried investors attempting to get hold of him. He ignored them all, finding a grain of comfort in the contempt he was now feeling for them for being so bloody greedy.But it was no recompense for the cold hard fact that he was now in big trouble and it would only take one of them to report him to the authorities and he'd be finished, if not in jail.

Come 4pm, routine dictated that he donned his running gear and took himself off for a jog from home around one of a number of circuits he'd worked out over the past couple of years, but today was no way a typical day and he certainly wasn't feeling up to a run. 'Hell, I might as well because at least it might clear my head,' he told himself.

Thirty minutes later, he'd reached the lake shore and was following his normal route through the Boulevard Parklands when the answer came to him. It was the worst possible solution, but he could think of no other. He'd just have to persuade his father and his uncle to cash in the valuable deeds to the firm's offices and adjoining small block of property in return for a twenty-five-year rent free lease. 'No, I can't possibly do that. There must be another way,' he told himself.

But as the next few days dragged on with a couple more answerphone messages from Charlie, which he could not bring himself to answer, Brad realised there was no other way.

Frank Meyer was mildly surprised when Brad called him up and asked if he could call in at the office after work the following afternoon, because they had not spoken for some time, following a mild falling out. The tone of his wayward son's, voice on the other end of the line, was enough to tell him all was not well.

The trouble with Brad was that he was too bright for his own good and was always coming up with ingenious money-making schemes, which somehow always involved a risk, or required some leap of faith. Frank had admitted this to his business partner and older brother

Joe on several occasions. So what had he been up to this time? he wondered.

The answer, when it came, was far worse than even he could have expected. He welcomed Brad into his spacious, richly furnished booklined office and offered him a drink, which his son accepted. They seated themselves opposite one another in two richly polished brown leather armchairs next to the large ornate marble surround fireplace. "So, what's this all about then son?" he asked. His heart beginning to thump, Brad quietly and calmly set out the whole story and the solution he'd arrived at.

His face now ashen white, Frank walked across to his desk and picked up the internal phone. "Joe, I'm glad you're still around. Can you come in here please?"

The shocked look on his brother's face, as he took the seat on the sofa facing them, and the undisguised one of anguish on that of his nephew's, told Joe that something had gone terribly wrong. "Brad, now tell your uncle what you've just told me."

Joe listened in growing disbelief as the young fool set out his story. Setting himself up as an investment consultant, without the experience of learning the profession with one of the investment houses, and ignoring all the examinations and other regulatory procedures was totally illegal. But then to go on offering share dealing advice on prospects that were becoming ever more risky, was sheer madness.

The problem was that his nephew was bright and had quickly learned the rules of the game and had clearly enjoyed more than a measure of success that had quickly drawn a growing following of investors. It only took one punter following Brad's advice to make a lot of money for the word to get around and that was clearly what had happened. Joe could feel his anger rising that this bloody young fool was about to wreck all he and his brother had worked for all these years, with both now holding high office in their legal profession associations. Any damage to the spotless reputation of Joseph B Meyer had to be stopped at all costs of that there was no doubt.

He took a deep breath to steady his nerves. "So even if we should agree to this solution of yours, how do you propose that we should proceed?" he asked with a measure of calm, he certainly did not feel.

Seeing a glimmer of light at the end of a very long and dark tunnel, Brad set out the plan that had been taking shape in his mind over the past couple of days.

"When these people contact me again, as they surely will the day after tomorrow, I am going to say that in order to take this matter forward, I'll fly down to Panama City or wherever else they are based in Central America to discuss my offer face to face."

Frank and Joe exchanged concerned glances. "I'm not sure it's such a good ideal to put yourself in harm's way Brad," his father said, again looking across at his brother for moral support.

"Even if they do attempt to besmirch our good name, we can easily distance ourselves from you and I am sure most all our clients and associates will not wish to punish the father for the sins of his son," he reasoned.

"Yes, that's true Frank, but it does not escape the central issue that these people want their six million dollars back and without totally cleaning ourselves out, there's no other way of doing this other than what Brad is proposing," Joe pointed out.

"Look Father and Uncle Frank, I probably wouldn't be putting myself in harm's way if I fly down and meet these people in some very public place, say an airport arrivals hall restaurant, before turning around, checking in, and flying back out again. But I will be asking for trouble if I simply ignore their demands."

A stony silence filled the room as both Joe and Frank thought about what Brad had said. Then Joe spoke again having now had a few more moments to gather his thoughts.

"There's no way we as a family are going to be bounced into this by these people, whoever they are. They were foolish enough to invest their cash with a client of yours, who simply took your advice, albeit poor advice, but it was their decision and not yours. When these people call back you must tell them straight that it's their problem and if they attempt to take any unlawful action against us, then we'll call in the appropriate federal agency," he said with an air of finality.

"But we'll be in a corner if they do call our bluff, brother because if we did report this matter to the appropriate authorities, then they'd pretty soon find out that Brad had been trading illegally and throw the book at him, which would probably mean a heavy fine or even imprisonment, and just think what that would do to our reputation?"

With the greatest reluctance, the brothers agreed to Brad's proposal that he should fly down to Central America and try and sort the matter out face to face because in truth, what else could they do?

4

Chapter 15

Brad had just come into his kitchen to fix himself some breakfast after yet another sleepless, night when the answerphone sparked into life and the same calm, measured voice filled the room. His first inclination was to answer the call and get this over with, but then changed his mind.

"Ah Sen Meyer, I am sorry to have missed you, so I will call again at around 4pm your time this afternoon and if you are still not in, then the same time the day after tomorrow." He paused and a car horn in the street below filled the silence.

"If there is still no* response, then I will have to call on you in person. It will not be an issue as Sen Jacobs has kindly provided us with your home address and also that of Joseph B Meyer and Sons. This would indeed be rather an inconvenience seeing that my associates and I are based in Bogota!" The line went dead.

Bloody hell, he could murder Harry, who was now obviously cooperating fully with these people to save his own skin and they'd clearly realised it was pointless going after him!

But there had been no actual threat, other than the implied one to harm the family firm's reputation, so maybe he should just go on ignoring this caller and if he did so, would he really trouble to fly all the way from Columbia to Toronto? There again, with six million dollars at stake, there was a strong possibility that this caller just might. Maybe, as a precaution, he should move out of the apartment and go to ground in a much more affordable one, somewhere out in the suburbs, until all this hopefully blew over. But that would not stop his father and uncle being paid a visit and there was no way he wanted that to happen.

Having lost his appetite completely, he retreated to the lounger in his study, with its bird's eye view over the city through the floor to ceiling window, and began turning everything over in his mind once again, but now from another angle.

Yes, he'd been an irresponsible fool to gamble on the markets with other people's money at stake. Most of his investors could afford to take a hit, which might in reality, only cancel out their earlier quite spectacular gains. But what of those who could not afford it and could now be in real hardship, although they had their own greed to blame? Perhaps he did owe a debt to these people and should contrive a way of paying them back. Maybe it hadn't been drug money, as Harry had suggested, because could he really believe anything that idiot had told him?

By lunchtime, Brad had decided he would take the next call and see what could be done to put things right and hopefully not by having to put the deeds to the firm's real estate on the line.

The call came through just after 4pm and this time he answered it, apologising for not being available earlier. "That's quiet all right, but I am glad that we are talking now Sen Meyer because, in truth, it would have been a nuisance to have had to fly to Toronto, so what do you have in mind for compensating my associates and I?"

Brad was conscious of taking a deep breath. "Firstly, I am not prepared to discuss this delicate matter over the telephone, and that, my friend, in non-negotiable. So, I'm proposing that we do meet up, but on some neutral ground," He paused. "Perhaps the café bar on the main concourse at Panama City International Airport, say at 2pm local time the day after tomorrow."

Brad had already checked and there was a flight arriving into Panama City's Tocumen International Airport at noon and another departing at 5pm. "As you wish, Sen Meyer. That is what we shall do, so how shall I recognise you?" he asked, "That's easy I'll be reading a copy of the Toronto Star."

All went far more smoothly than Brad had anticipated with the flight, taking off and landing on time. He now perceived himself to be in the driving seat, having called the shots over setting up the meeting and was feeling reasonably secure in his choice of places, because if anyone tried to muscle him off the airport concourse, he'd kick up one hell of a fuss.

The immaculately dressed, middle-aged man, who took the café bar stool opposite, slid an embossed business card across the table announcing himself as Developments Consultant Edelmira Sanchez. He was olive skinned, of slight build, and the moment he spoke, Brad knew this was the person who'd contacted him.

"You certainly have a talent for spotting excellent prospects and it's just unfortunate you got your last tip so disastrously wrong," he said after they'd participated in a little banal small talk about how quiet the airport seemed to be at this hour.

The unexpected commiseration caught Brad by surprise. Perhaps there was no drug related money laundering operation and that had been a figment of Harry Jacob's fertile imagination when forced into a corner.

"Look Brad, I hope I may call you Brad, as I assured you earlier, we're all reasonable men and I think there may be an amicable way out of this small difficulty," he suggested. "Do you have something in mind Sen Sanchez?" Brad asked, his heart beginning to race.

The caller casually stirred the coffee around in the cup, he'd brought to the table with him, as if he was carefully considering his reply. "As a matter of fact, we have," he said, after a few moments. "Our organisation could do with a young man of your obvious talents because in that way we would avoid getting our fingers burnt as we did with Sen Jacobs."

For a moment, Brad was tempted to ask how they had come across Harry, but then thought better of it.

"We are, we recognise, a little parochial in our outlook when it comes to world-wide investment opportunities," Sen Sanchez admitted. "So, it would be refreshing, and I am sure, more profitable, to work with someone with a more international understanding of the investment world," he suggested.

"Sen Sanchez, I think you should know that I am entirely self-taught and have not come up through the ranks of one of the established investment houses. He did not add that he'd been acting totally illegally by choosing to ignore all the regulatory procedures put in place by the federal government to discourage rogue trading.

"That maybe so, but it has clearly set you free to think without too many preconceived ideas, which you have done with an incredible amount of success over the past nine months until the recent regrettable incident." He paused for another sip of his coffee. "My associates and I need a partner with a roving brief to trawl world markets in all commodities and to seek out those special investment opportunities, a talent you clearly have," he pointed out.

"Sen Sanchez, I have to ask the obvious question and that concerns the source of these, I'm assuming, substantial funds, you have to invest," he said, suddenly catching sight of a movement out of the corner of his eye.

"Papa there you are!" Approaching from their right, was an attractive young woman in Denims and a matching floral top carrying a large folder, tucked under one arm.

"Francesca, aren't we supposed to be meeting back at the apartment?" Sen Sanchez responded, caught off his guard.

"Yes Papa, but I thought if I met you here, we could go straight on for an early supper," she replied, locking eyes with Brad and instantly liking what she saw. "I called your office and they told me this was where I'd find you," she explained.

"May I introduce my daughter, who is studying at the university here in Panama City, which was why your suggestion that we meet here rather than back home in Bogota was particularly fortunate," he explained.

"Francesca, this is Sen Brad Meyer, who has flown down from Toronto to discuss some business." Again their eyes locked.

"Are you staying over, Sen Meyer, because if so, perhaps you would like to join us for dinner, if that is OK with you Papa?" she asked. "It would be fine with me because Sen Meyer and I have still to conclude our business" he answered. "But I hope you won't be talking work all evening especially as we don't manage to meet up that often."

Brad's mind went into overdrive. Was this a honey trap to entice him away from the relative safety of the airport concourse? So, what the hell should he do now? The sensible plan was to hear what Sen Sanchez had to say and fly home.

Instead, he told them he was due to board a return flight in a couple of hours, but could postpone until the following afternoon if necessary. He was intrigued to hear what deal was being proposed and his instincts told him all would be OK.

"That's settled then, so let's go," said Francesca, leading the way out to her flashy white convertible just a couple of hundred yards away in a short stay car park. Not the motor one would normally associate with a student, Brad thought.

"I suffer from over indulgence when it comes to my daughter, Sen Meyer," Edelmira said, noting the look of surprise on his face. There was a jumbled pile of books on the front passenger seat, so they both climbed into the back. The books were a reassuring sign that this was not a set up and allowed Brad to relax just a little.

She'd booked an upmarket restaurant in its own secluded walled garden because it was where they always ate when he came to visit and it was quite close to her apartment.

Brad was surprised how busy it was, seeing it was only just after 5pm and began to relax because if he was going to be abducted then why would they have gone to all this bother? He was made even more at ease when father and daughter were greeted by the owner and he was introduced as a business associate who had just flown in from Toronto. They ate grilled fish with a large salad and began trading life stories, which put Brad even more at his ease.

The Sanchez family, he learned, hailed from the pacific coast of Costa Rica where they had a small estate and Francesca was raised by her father and his extended family following the tragic death of her mother from breast cancer in her early forties. Francesca had followed the traditional gap year student routes around the world and both she and Brad began swapping tales about their experiences in India, Thailand, Vietnam and other exotic places where their paths might have crossed.

But her gap year had become three, after she'd become well and truly hooked on travelling and had taken a host of summer jobs. She'd been a chalet maid in the Austrian alps, crewed for a holiday sailing company in the Greek islands and finally, become a cocktail waitress with a Miami based cruise line, whose ships operated around the world.

Eventually, she'd exhausted her desire for travel and succumbed to her father's gentle insistence that she return home and finish her education or find herself some meaningful career.

"I won't bore you with all the details, but I eventually opted for this really interesting three-year university economics course here in Panama City and am now waiting for my finals results." she said.

"I'm hoping my daughter is going to join me in business, but I think she has other ideas of a more social nature," said Edelmira.

"Let's not talk about that now, Papa," she retorted, a small note of annoyance in her voice.

Her father, Brad noted, was far more circumspect about his professional life, other than he was a senior member of a development corporation based in the Columbian capital which had interests throughout the Caribbean, Central and South America.

"So, are we going to offer Brad our guest room or do we find a hotel for him the night Papa?" asked Francesca, right out of the blue.

There was a directness to her, which Brad found refreshing, seeing that the modus operandi while growing up back home had been to wander all around the houses rather than coming straight to the point. "I think that's up to Brad to decide, but staying with us might be useful in that it would give us an opportunity to conclude our business arrangements," he replied.

Brad was now totally convinced he was no longer in any danger and finding out more about these 'business arrangements' was beginning to intrigue him.

The family's modern apartment turned out to be only a couple of streets away. Francesca occupied the penthouse suite with its tiled rooftop views, wide veranda, hot tub and array of sun loungers and furled parasols. It was mentioned in passing that Papa owned the whole block and that she was nominally supposed to keep an eye on things, which was more of a token responsibility, seeing there was also management company which reported direct to him. Francesca showed Brad to the guest suite, equipped like a five-star hotel bedroom with obligatory white robe and slippers, neatly folded towels and luckily, a range of expensive toiletries in the floor to ceiling tiled and mirrored bathroom. She excused herself saying it had been a long day and she was going to have a bath and an early night and that Papa was asking that he joined him for a nightcap out on the patio.

Brad took a shower to freshen up and wandered out onto the wide patio, with its array of tubs filled with exotic shrubs, and found Edelmira already relaxing in the warm evening sun. He accepted a whisky served with ice and they chinked glasses.

"Well today certainly hasn't turned out in the way I expected," Brad admitted. "And how had you anticipated it would pan out?" Edelmira responded, putting him right on the spot. Brad hesitated. "I was thinking you would be wanting to know just how I intended compensating you and your colleagues for your unfortunate loss, and that by now I'd be close to touching down in Toronto," he replied. "I think we might have touched on that already," said Edelmira, gently swirling the spirit around in his chunky cut glass tumbler. "As I explained earlier, my associates and I now feel we require someone 'in house,' I think that is the term you use, to help us invest the profits from our various enterprises," he said. "And exactly what are these enterprises, Edelmira?" Brad asked quietly.

He'd switched to using Sen Sanchez's Christian name at some point during their relaxed conversations with Francesca earlier in the evening. "We have interests in mining, petrochemicals, the construction industry, real estate, entertainment and the gaming industry," he revealed.

"Over the years we have supported politicians favouring democracy and free enterprise throughout Central and South America, if we believed they had prospects for success in their endeavours. To that end, we have an extremely well briefed political analyst, who studies these matters and advises us in these areas. He mostly always gives sound advice, but just occasionally he will get it wrong, as you did recently, and we'll have backed a man who closes the door on us as soon as he's in power. As I am sure you can imagine, the result of these endeavours, has given us a position of considerable influence over the years," said Edelmira.

Now he was looking up into the warm night sky where a full moon was almost overhead.

"Are you perhaps suggesting that my role might be to search for new investment opportunities in the same way that your other analyst keeps a close watch on the political situation in this part of the world?" he asked. "Brad that is exactly what we are proposing," Edelmira responded. "So would I be able to fulfil this role working out of my office in Toronto?" Edelmira slowly shook his head. "Sadly no, because we prefer our people to be inhouse and in country, but I am sure that would not inconvenience you, given what you said earlier, about your love of travel and a little adventure. But you'd certainly not be spending all the time at your desk because we also encourage our people to take a close on the spot interest in our various enterprises," he assured Brad. "I have to admit this sounds the perfect role for me, but what have you in mind by way of remuneration, bearing in mind the small matter of the six million dollars?" he asked.

"We don't penalise Aldo when, despite our considerable investment in a particular politician, it all turns sour, so I guess that if you accept this role, the same would apply to you, if my associates agree." He hesitated. "And, of course, you would be handsomely rewarded for your endeavours," he added.

We've a board meeting in Bogota, three days from now so maybe it would be a good idea for you to attend, unless you have any other pressing engagements," he suggested. "I haven't, but I didn't even bring an overnight bag, so I only have the clothes I stand up in and no shaving essentials," he pointed out. "That's no problem. I'm sure Francesca would be happy to take you shopping tomorrow," he added.

They bid one another goodnight and Brad returned to his room, his head in a spin with a growing sense of excited anticipation accompanied by the nagging feeling that the situation was moving far too fast and that he was being caught up and swept along by it. This whole business of backing politicians in exchange for future favours and influence was concerning. But then the rogue streak in his personality justified that as being simply the way of the world and who was he to take the moral high ground anyway? Then the delightful prospect of being taken shopping by the lovely Francesca only served to fuel his excitement for all that might lay ahead. Perhaps Harry Jacobs had done him a favour after all, he thought as he fell into a deep sleep.

Chapter 16

"Here in Panama City business casual is normal, but in Bogota they're more conservative, so we'll have to find you a couple of business suits to match and then we'll look for some casual gear, not to mention anything else you may need," said Francesca as they drove lazily through the city traffic, the following. morning. She was wearing a floral dress, but he couldn't help noticing her sun browned legs, especially when she changed gear and the material rode up above her knees.

Brad had never been particularly interested in clothes and shopping for them was far more an inconvenience than a pleasure, so as long as he felt reasonably turned out as the occasion required, then that was OK. It was the reason why he tended to wear the same clothes until even he could see it was time for a change. But Francesca was far more interested in what she wore and was now relishing the opportunity to dress a man, perhaps her man if all went well.

She'd already started weighing him up as a likely prospect that had suddenly and unexpectedly landed in her world. The shopping took most of the day and for once, Brad was really enjoying himself. It was interspersed with trips back to the car to lock an

assortment of bags and packages into the boot before setting off again. It was not that they'd gone over the top on this unexpected shopping spree, but that Francesca was never happy for him to buy the first garment that looked the part, which he'd initially found a little frustrating given his normal purchasing habit.
But then he'd decided to relax and go with the flow because who would not when their dresser was a highly attractive young woman, who was clearly enjoying the experience.
They grabbed lunch at a street café, having earlier taken a break for coffee, and by mid-afternoon they'd finally finished.
"I'm going to need a roomy case for all this stuff," he said, as they made their final trip back to the car. They both stopped dead in their tracks and burst out laughing. A suitcase was the one essential item they'd forgotten to buy. Making a u turn, they headed back to the store they'd just left, but this time Francesca grabbed his hand. The happy sunny day he'd spent with Charlie, only a few short weeks before, had conveniently parked itself somewhere in the recesses of his mind until this moment and he suddenly felt a twinge of guilt!
Twenty hours later, he and Edelmira were on a short one hour and forty-five-minute flight hop to Bogota. They

landed in late afternoon and Edelmira dropped him off at a small hotel, which he and his associates used to accommodate incoming guests, and said he would pick him up again around 10am to accompany him to the group's monthly board meeting.

"You'll be well looked after here because we own this property and it's staffed by our people, so if there's anything you need then just ask. Oh! and the tab will be looked after," he explained.

The hotel had been built in the colonial era and Brad was shown to a large second floor room with tall windows opening out onto an internal courtyard where the splashing from an ornate central fountain drifted up to him.

A fan lazily beat the air overhead as he unpacked his new case and hung his two suits in a heavy wooden wardrobe.

It looked as if it had stood there since the hotel was built, he thought. Then he kicked off his shoes and lay down on the big bed, which had probably also been there as long as the wardrobe. He would go down later for some supper, but now he just wanted some time to think. So much had happened over the past forty-eight roller coaster hours.

When he'd left Toronto, he was on a damage limitation exercise to see how best to extricate himself from a potential six-million-dollar debt. But now it seemed to have been unexpectedly waived away in exchange for an advisory role within this still shadowy corporation, and he'd met a most attractive girl into the bargain, but what sort of bargain was he making here?

Again, he had the nagging feeling that he was being swept along and into the arms of an organisation, which might well demand ever more from him, and that his best plan was to get the hell out of there while he still could. But surely, he'd passed the point of no return when he boarded the flight with Edelmira earlier that afternoon. They'd spoken little while in the air, but clearly Francesca's obvious liking for Brad had not gone unnoticed and he got the impression that her father was going to do little to discourage it. From that brief father-daughter conversation about her choice of a career, Brad began to speculate that if he joined the organisation, then perhaps Edelmira was vaguely thinking that she might follow! But with or without Francesca, did he really want to spend the next couple of years, or maybe longer, far from home as a well-paid cog in someone else's wheel?

No. He valued his independence and that had to be his bottom line.

So that being the case, might he be able to buy his way into a slice of their action by using the deeds to Joseph B Meyer's valuable real estate as collateral? After all, both his father and Uncle Joe had already indicated they might be prepared to go along with the idea, if it was the only way of getting both him and the good name of the family firm off the hook, he rationalized.

Edelmira picked him up on time, but instead of driving towards the city centre, as he'd expected they would, they appeared to be heading out of town in his smart top of the range black Lincoln Continental. Yet another sign of the family's obvious wealth. It was not a long drive but, as before on the flight, Edelmira spoke little, other than to explain that the corporation's headquarters was set in extensive grounds in the midst of a banana plantation. "We grow a lot of bananas here in Columbia, but it's mostly all coffee, as I am sure you are aware, plus cocoa, tobacco, sugarcane and all the other traditional crops found in this part of the world," he explained.

A slow twenty-minute dusty drive through the plantation, where harvesting was in progress with open trucks full of fruit also using the road, brought them to a huge pair of ornate gates, pulled open by two security guards in light green uniforms.

'No turning back now,' thought Brad, as they passed through and up a manicured drive towards a hacienda style mansion and spread of buildings. Pulling up in a shady parking area, they walked across to the main house, clearly built by a plantation owner as an opulent demonstration of his wealth.

Entering an hotel size marble floored foyer, they approached an ornate wooden table where a young woman sat.

"Good morning, Gabriella. Will you show Sen Meyer here into the drawing room and make him a coffee, or perhaps a soft drink if he prefers," he instructed.

"I expect it will be getting on for an hour before I come down and collect you Brad," Edelmira said, putting a fatherly hand on his shoulder, before turning on his heels. It was another small sign that he was already part of this enterprise, whether he liked it or not.

The call came earlier than expected and Edelmira was showing him into a large meeting room on the first floor where seven heads turned to meet his gaze. They were all middle-aged men, wearing suits, who greeted him with friendly interest, after he was shown to an empty seat half way along the boardroom style table and introduced by Edelmira, who'd taken the vacated place opposite. It was clear he'd already brought the gathering up to speed with regard to the position, but what had not been apparent up until then, was that Edelmira was obviously the chairman of this group.

It had been Brad's intention to put forward his proposal for acquiring a stake, albeit a modest one, in this obviously massively lucrative multi-faceted enterprise, but now, seeing that Edelmira was actually the one in the driving seat, he was having second thoughts. Surely it would be far more diplomatic to share the idea with him first, not only out of courtesy, but because he'd be able to suggest the best options.

"Firstly, I must thank you all, and especially Sen Sanchez, for offering me this valuable opportunity of becoming associated with your enterprise," said Brad, when invited to say a few words. "Clearly, there's going to be a lot for me to absorb before I'll be in a position to know how best to assist you and finally to commit myself to your endeavours, but suffice to say, I am really interested." The nods of approval from around the table suggested that his small stalling speech had gone down well and he was invited to join them later for lunch.

Leaving the room, he made his way slowly down the wide staircase, peering casually at the random collection of paintings as he descended. Modern works of an abstract nature seemed to be placed alongside vaguely familiar oils in heavy ornate frames. He was certainly no art connoisseur, because if he had been, he'd have quickly realised there was a small fortune hanging on those old lath and plaster walls.

"Is it OK if I take a wander around the grounds?" he asked Gabriella, once he was back in the foyer. "There's not really much to see, but there is a garden if you go out through the conservatory," she said in perfect English, pointing toward a hallway opposite. The conservatory was large with a collection of exotic plants in huge terracotta pots and he noticed a table being laid for lunch as he walked past, but there were only four places, which he found a bit odd.

"Sen Meyer there is a telephone call for you," the receptionist interrupted before he'd had chance to step outside. There's only one person that could be,' he thought, turning and following her back to the reception where he was handed the heavy black receiver.

"I just thought I'd see how you were getting along with Papa and his friends," said Francesca. Brad told her he was really pleased she'd called, but he'd only had a brief meeting with her father and his associates and he hoped to learn more from them over lunch. "So, which of the two suits we chose are you wearing today? I bet it was the lighter one," she added. "How right you are," he replied, although it was the wrong answer, but there was no need to disappoint her because she'd never know. It was only a small untruth, but like so many others he'd told when he didn't think it mattered. or knew he was highly unlikely to be caught out.

Being a little economical with the truth, when it suited, had long ago become second nature to Brad Meyer because as long as no one got hurt, did it really matter? The trouble was that, by and by, small untruths could grow into larger and more deceitful ones, which could always be made justifiable in one way or another, and now he was poised to take this philosophy to a whole new level! "Call me tonight so that you can tell me all about your day," she said before ringing off as the unmistakeable beating sound of an approaching helicopter filled the air. Retracing his steps through the conservatory, he stood looking out into the garden and watched as the chopper dropped out of sight behind a cluster of giant pines. It remained on the ground for a few minutes before rising quickly into the air again and disappearing. He was about to step out into the garden when Edelmira called and he turned to find him and two of his associates standing by the luncheon table, the other four, he guessed, had just departed.

"Brad, may I introduce you to my close friends and business partners Lucas Martinez and Antonio Garcia, who are both based here with me at the Hacienda Jimarenal during the week."

Lucas, the shorter and stockier of the two, was the first step forward and shake Brad warmly by the hand followed by Antonio, who was lean, immaculately dressed and whose welcome appeared just a little more circumspect.

Over lunch he learned how, starting from small beginnings some twenty years earlier, Jimarenal and Associates had begun slowly acquiring companies with real growth potential, putting in strong management teams with a large degree of autonomy and then moving on and that was still their modus operandi. There were currently some thirty companies within the portfolio and it was Antonio and Lucas's role to keep a watching brief over them. Both had apartments in the grounds and were in residence at least three days a week, unless flying off to meet with company bosses around the group.

Again, Brad was sorely tempted to ask where all the cash came from to fund this on-going acquisition programme, but drew back reasoning this would all come clear later.

Maybe they borrowed on the increased value generated by their involvement in the previous acquisition, he reasoned. But the problem with that pyramid style operation was that it could quickly collapse in any real downturn. Then there was this questionable practice of supporting up and coming politicians in the various countries where they operated, obviously in return for favours when they reached positions of influence, as Edelmira had so matter of factually revealed earlier. That clearly smacked of corruption, so that even he could not help himself reluctantly coming to the conclusion that all was definitely not as it seemed, but in some perverse way it excited him.

"Just a random question, I know Edelmira, but how did your organisation come to be called Jimarenal and Associates?" Brad asked during a suitable pause in the conversation. "That's easily explained. My family have a small estate close to Puerto Jimanez, down on the Pacific coast of Costa Rica, where I spent my childhood. It is still my escape when time allows. And the friend with whom I launched this business, but is no longer with us, happened to come from a small town not far from Mount Arenal the country's most active volcano," he explained.

Brad wondered whether the friend who 'was no longer with us' had died, or simply left the organisation. Again, he did not pursue it, but judged the time might now be right to make a proposal mixed with a rich cocktail of excitement and guilt!

All three listened attentively as he laid out his proposal for earning a small stake in the venture, by offering up as collateral, the freehold on the valuable real estate owned by Joseph B Meyer back home in Toronto. He indicated that he was sure that both his father and his uncle would be interested in a back seat involvement and content for him to look after their interest, which was of course a complete lie.

"So Brad what would this capital investment be worth and what interest would your family want in return?" Edelmira asked quietly.

"I'm guessing around ten million US dollars, but we would not want it to disappear into your general melting pot."

Now he could see he had their full attention. "So, what exactly are you proposing?" Edelmira asked. Taking a deep breath, Brad outlined the plan that had been formulating in his fertile mind over the last twenty-four hours.

"When we spoke earlier, you outlined the broad scope of your investment interests here in central and South America and the Caribbean, but you did not mention hotels, which I believe are definitely going to be one of the big growth sectors," he revealed. "And why is that?" Lucas asked. "Because budget holidays for the masses, made possible by the new jet aircraft, have really taken off in the United States and across the pond in Europe. As you may know, Pan American introduced overseas flights operating Boeing 707 and Douglas DC-8 jetliners in the late 1950s and it's incredible how this market has expanded over the past five years and I have a strong feeling it's only going to grow and grow," he told them. "You seem to know quite a lot about this," Antonio remarked. "That's because I was asked to look at the growth potential for this sector by one of my investment clients only a couple of months ago and it was really brought home to me on a recent visit to the UK on another matter only a few weeks ago. Believe me, the Brits have really gone for this in their thousands with cheap flights to the new up and coming Spanish resorts. So my proposal would be to launch a new brand of affordable, but smart hotels, maybe starting in the Caribbean to begin soaking up some of this holiday traffic coming from the US. My plan would be to buy up two or three, maybe rundown properties, say on the Caribbean coast of Costa Rica, give them a makeover and perhaps link up with an airline and offer package deals," he suggested.

"This would all be a bit of a learning curve, but I'm pretty sure we'd see our money back with interest fairly quickly," he predicted. It was clear he had them interested, but again it was Antonio who was first with a question. "If you're so sure this is going to work, why do you need us Sen Meyer? Why don't you and your family just go off and paddle your own canoe?"

The fact that he'd addressed Brad formally, signalled that he was not as ready as Edelmira, or indeed the far more friendly Lucas, to accept this investor, who had already caused the organisation to lose a significant amount of money. His was a searching question which was going to take some careful answering because, never in a million years, would his father or uncle allow him to go off and gamble with their valuable and hard-earned real estate.

"To start with, I do feel somewhat responsible for your recent loss, albeit it was through a third party, and it would be a far more comfortable prospect to launch this new venture with the added security of you and your associates behind it," he countered. "Also, I understand from all I have been told, that your organisation has a certain amount of political influence which might be brought to bear. This could well prove invaluable when we move from taking over existing properties to building new ones in prime and pristine coastal areas, which have yet to be developed, and over which there could well be some local resistance to our job and wealth creating progress."

Edelmira thanked Brad for a most interesting proposal. "Perhaps you might like to stay on here in one of our guest apartments and work this proposal up into a positive development plan to submit to our board," Edelmira suggested.

"We meet a week today and have people in San Jose who would certainly be able to advise and assist us with this most interesting project." It was more of an instruction than a suggestion. "Gabriella will show you to one if our suites and I'll have her prepare all the information we have which could be helpful in your research."

Brad sensed a certain distancing between himself and the man whose Panama apartment he'd shared for two nights and whose daughter had taken him on a clothes buying day out.

Getting to his feet, he thanked them for lunch and made his way back along the wide tile floored hallway to the reception.

Chapter 17

"As you are going to be staying with us for a few days Sen Meyer, I'd better show you around," Gabriella said, rising and coming out from behind her reception desk. She was tall, he'd say too thin, with long black hair, tied away from her face and dressed in a dark business suit and probably in her early twenties and there were no rings on her fingers.

He followed her out through a side door and towards a cluster of clearly former stable buildings, set around three sides of a large central courtyard, which had all been converted into apartments.

She was carrying a bronze metal key, which she inserted into the heavy pine door of the nearest apartment, throwing it open and casting a wedge of bright sunlight into the darkened interior. "Wait here a moment Sen Meyer while I open the shutters," she instructed. "There you are, now I can show you around, but first perhaps you could fix the fasteners," she called through the open space as the two long green window shades suddenly swung out towards him. "This place is well equipped," he commented as she showed him around and he thought of the guest room he'd been given at Edelmira and Francesca's luxurious apartment back in Panama City. Again, there was a large tiled bathroom, separate double bedroom and spacious lounge, but this time, it came complete with a desk and accompanying chair, a thick pad of paper, typewriter and a black telephone. This was clearly where he was to work up his new hotels division proposal for Edelmira and his associates. Gabriella walked across to the telephone and picked up its small directory.

"You'll always get me on zero and if you need anything from me after hours just dial double zero," she instructed. "Oh, so you also live on site do you?" he asked, ignoring the inuendo that he was sure was not intended. "Yes, I have the apartment at the far end of the block and no doubt I will see you for supper in the conservatory, which is at 8pm," she said. "The other extension numbers here are for Edelmira, Antonio and Lucas, although they're not always around, plus Francisco and Chuck, who mostly always are. Francisco is our General Manager. He is responsible for the smooth running of the entire hacienda operation, including overseeing our chef and his two assistants and our four housekeepers, who we certainly need when we're hosting conferences and other events for people from our associate companies," she explained. "So, what does Chuck do?" Brad asked. "He's our Head of Security and is in charge of all those aspects here on the enclosed hacienda estate, including our four gardeners, who keep the place tidy and tend our fruit and vegetable plots, and on the greater banana plantation, which covers many hectares and is far more open to the outside world," she explained.

"That all sounds quite an operation," Brad replied. "Yes, and believe me it is. Oh, and there will probably be two others dining with us, namely our pilots, whose helicopters are housed in a hanger just along the service road behind here," she said turning and closing the door behind him.

Brad took off his shoes and lay down on the bed to think about the enclosed, and clearly closely controlled world, he'd so easily allowed himself to enter and which now might be not be quite so easy to leave should he wish to. Still, he should definitely go along with the situation as it was presenting itself at the moment, because this really was the most intriguing set up. But first and most importantly, just how was he going to persuade his father and uncle to hand over the deeds to their real estate in exchange for a long lease? After all. he stood to inherit a large part of it one day anyway, he rationalised.

He must have drifted off to sleep for a few minutes

before being disturbed by a loud knock on the door, which he hurriedly climbed off the bed and opened. "Sen Meyer, Gabriella has asked me to bring you over these papers." With that, the pretty young woman, handed the bundle over to him, turned and walked away. He guessed she was one of the housekeeping team just running an errand; but no doubt he'd find out later. Carrying the papers back over to the desk, he sat down and started going slowly through them, but quickly realised they were not going to be of much help. They were mostly all in Spanish, as were the various newspaper articles, with the dull print grey faces of politicians, who were those being supported by the organisation, he supposed. No, this stuff was not going to be of any use unless he had an enthusiastic Spanish and English-speaking associate to interpret them and to generally help with his endeavours. He thought immediately of Francesca.

She was now at a loose end, having finished her finals and he got the sense during their day together that she was searching around for a new direction. He also knew that Edelmira wanted her to become involved with his business, but up until now, she had been resisting the idea. So, might her father welcome this as the perfect opportunity for changing his daughter's mind, seeing that he must have sensed the attraction between them.

If Francesca did agree to helping him and it all worked out on a business and personal level, surely this would be his fast track to the top of this organisation and to all the trappings of wealth that went with it.

Tentatively raising the idea with his prospective father-in-law had to be the way forward, because if he was in any way opposed to the prospect then, it would be dead in the water!

In any case, there was no other way to go because, as he suddenly realised, he had no way of contacting her at the moment.

Walking over to the main house around 7.45pm, in the casual gear he and Francesca had so happily chosen together, he had the strange sensation of being the new boy at supper time in some upmarket public school, not that he'd ever been near such a place.

"There you are Sen Meyer," said Gabriella, who had, he guessed, been loitering in the wide side entrance hallway waiting to escort him in to the conservatory. She was wearing a black trouser suit with her long black hair tied back off her face and looking for all the world as if she'd just stepped right off the page of a fashion magazine. In short, she was stunning!

Then to his even greater surprise, she took him by the arm and propelled him gently into the conservatory where she introduced him to all the team members, she'd described earlier that afternoon. But to his quiet disappointment, neither Edelmira, nor Lucas or Antonio, were there!

Everyone seemed to be generally in a good mood as if this was the time they relaxed after busy days. It gave him the distinct impression they shared an unspoken camaraderie, as if they were all members of some exclusive club.

From quite early on in his life, Brad had inherited a heightened sense of intuitiveness, which he'd found both an advantage and a disadvantage as he grew to maturity. Now he was sensing a menace in this space, as if all those present were party to some secret that had yet to be shared with him and the feeling grew as the evening progressed, quietly fuelled by the odd remark, here and there along the way.

An extensive hot and cold buffet had been laid out on a long table and after he and Gabriella had helped themselves to a first course, she led him to a table currently being occupied by Francisco, the General Manager and Chuck, the security chief, who both looked as if they were more than capable of taking care of themselves.

"So, Sen Meyer is not Gabriella the perfect hostess?" Francisco remarked when they were seated. It sounded just a little condescending and by now he sensed she was certainly not the kind of woman who would tolerate that if it had been so.

"Yes, I assist Francisco as organiser and hostess when we have our regular meetings of associates, who stay at our hotel in town and bussed out here for the occasions," she responded by way of an explanation. Chuck, he learned, was a veteran of the Korean War and had been a mercenary for several years before finding his way to the Hacienda Jimarenel by a circuitous route, he did not trouble to explain.

He left half way through the evening saying he had some business to attend to, but not before promising he'd swing by the main entrance around 10am and take Brad on a tour of the property to get his bearings. His place was soon taken by Michael, one of the two helicopter pilots, who Brad quickly learned was also a Korean War veteran and a friend of Chuck's, the other pilot being a local man, who'd flown Antonio and Lucas over into neighbouring Ecuador to attend to some business that afternoon and were not expected back for a couple of days.

So, did that mean Edelmira was still around and, if so, why had he not shown up? Both Michael and Francisco soon made their excuses and went their separate ways leaving Brad alone with Francesca, who showed no sign that she was going anywhere soon. "It's nice to have some different company," she said, asking if he wanted another cold beer, but saying she was OK herself. "It's all pretty full on here most of the time, but then on evenings like these, when it's just the regular crew, I get a little tired of their company, so mostly help myself to what I want and take it back to my apartment," she admitted.

"I'm honoured, and indeed grateful, that you showed up for me," he said. "No, you'd have been all right, and seeing you're here as Edelmira's guest, they'd have made you especially welcome," she assured him.

She, he learned, had been part of the Hacienda 'family' for some years and had gradually made herself a key player in the organisation, even acting as hotel General Manager for a short spell, but had declined when Edelmira had offered her the full-time role. "It's hard enough to escape from here as is," she said, without offering any further explanation.

It was just another of those small remarks that concerned him, although he felt it wiser not to pursue it. "Talking of Edelmira, I had hoped to have a brief talk with him about those papers you sent over earlier, but he's not joined us this evening," he remarked. "No, he mostly prefers to dine alone in his own apartments, often with Antonio and Lucas if they're around, but I can ask if he could spare you a few minutes because Michael's flying him off to join them first thing in the morning." Edelmira occupied a suite of rooms on the first floor, overlooking the front of the hacienda, and was sitting in his white shirt sleeves at a heavy and highly ornate wooden desk, illuminated by a blue shaded lamp, when Gabriella accompanied him into the room, turned and left. Coming out from behind the desk, he waved Brad into one of two comfortable leather arm chairs set either side of an elaborate fireplace. The room was book-lined with a long boardroom style table on the far side and, he guessed, was the epicentre of this organisation.

"Now Brad how can I help?" he asked, coming straight to the point and without any preliminary small-talk about how he was settling in. It was as if the atmosphere between them had completely changed from that of the friendly chat they'd shared after Francesca had kissed her father goodnight and left them alone together.

Maybe this was his natural demeanor when not being around the daughter he clearly doted upon, or perhaps he'd interrupted him in the middle of something important and under normal circumstances he'd never have been allowed up so late in the evening.

"Look Edelmira I'm sorry to have troubled you because it seems to me as if you are in the middle of some important work and that my interruption is clearly not helpful. Gabriella tells me you are away early in the morning, so what I have to say can clearly wait upon your return."

It was as if the directness of his response had suddenly released a tension as he watched his prospective father-in-law, visibly relax in front of him. Brad suddenly had the unerring feeling that few of his associates would have had the temerity to address him in such a direct way, but that he'd succeeded because the most important person in Edelmira's life had taken a shine to him.

"I apologise for forgetting my manners. Yes, you are right, I am in the middle of something important, but that was no reason for my rudeness, so let's have a nightcap," he suggested, rising slowly from his chair and reaching towards a whisky decanter and two chunky cut glasses. Brad said again the matter he wanted to discuss really could wait for a more convenient time, but Edelmira now waved his suggestion away.

This was now surely the moment to put all his cards on the table and just how it would all pan out, for all his intuitiveness, he could not be certain. If he was wrong and there was nothing vaguely corrupt at the centre of the Jimarenel organisation, then this would surely be sayonara, but if he was right, then there could be everything to play for! He took a deep breath.

"Firstly, I do have a confession to make in that neither my father nor my uncle will willingly swap the deeds to their real estate for a long-term lease, unless they truly believe that I will be put seriously in harm's way if they do not.

Now you will ask what sort of man would even contemplate cheating on his own father. Such a man can have not a single shred of honour, you will surely say. But like much else in life, as I am sure you will know, things are not always as they seem. To start with, I am not my father's son. I am the result of my mother's little indiscretion, just a week before her wedding, and which they have chosen to keep secret from me and are still under the impression that I do not know. Indiscretions, even as momentous as this one can and will often be forgiven over the passage of time, but my stepfather has been incapable of forgiveness and has punished my mother by a coldness to me that has haunted our relationship ever since I was a child.

So, as he and my uncle will have left this world by the time the lease expires and I will have probably inherited at least half the estate, I can see no real harm in what I am proposing and besides, if I use the perceived value of the real estate wisely with the building of a successful hotel chain and other endeavours, then I plan to be in a position to repay the family in any event, he revealed. A silence filled the space between them, broken only by some exotic night bird call drifting in through the half open window.

"You are right," Edelmira agreed in a low voice, toying with his whisky tumbler. "Things in the business world and beyond are seldom as they seem and that is a sentiment with which I can whole heartedly agree. Yours will be a small deceit which we can accommodate in the great scheme of things and is something you can leave me to take care of. He paused. So what is the other matter you wish to discuss?"

Brad took a deep breath.

"When I looked through the papers you had sent over for me to read this afternoon, it became clear to me that, not speaking Spanish, a deficiency I intend to remedy by the way, and not being familiar with any of the customs or formalities of doing business in your part of the world, what I would really need would be an intelligent and enthusiastic associate and confidant," he said, looking at Edemira straight in the eye as man to man.

"And you think my daughter would be ideal for the roll?" Edelmira said quietly, now fixing Brad with a look which gave not the smallest hint of what was going on in his mind.

"Yes, I do sir," replied Brad. It was almost as if he was asking a father for his daughter's hand in marriage.

A long silence filled the space between them into, which more nocturnal sounds, drifted in through the window on the warm evening air.

Without saying another word, Edelmira slowly put down his tumbler, got to his feet and walked over and closed the window, as if he wished to be sure they were completely alone.

"And what does Francesca think about this idea? he asked quietly, without turning back into the room.

"Naturally I would never have dreamed of raising it with her without seeking your view, and hopefully approval. She did call me earlier to ask how I was settling in, but it was before I'd even seen the papers, so the prospect had not even occurred to me."

Edelmira knew full well that his daughter had called because all visitors to the hacienda had their bedroom phones tapped as a matter of security.

It was clear to him, there was a natural attraction between them and the idea of his formally foot lose daughter being encouraged into his fold of her own will, because that was indeed the only way it was going to happen, clearly had its appeal.

Edelmira had slowly imposed almost total control over his organisation over the years by his force of will, but he knew that would never apply to Francesca because like him, she was totally her own person.

Returning, he picked up his tumbler, from which very little of the whisky had been sipped, and continued toying with it, clearly deep in thought. "All right Brad, you have, it seems, been open and honest with me, which I respect, and in return I am going to level with you." He paused, as if choosing his words carefully.

"Like you, I have over the years become irritated when goals I have wished to achieve have been made more difficult by petty officialdom, politicians appealing to the masses, while quietly feathering their own nests and others with vested interests stubbornly refusing to see my point of view. So, as you decided to set yourself up as an investment consultant without following any of the rules, I have taken a similar pathway in life' using the natural forces of persuasion in their many forms to ensure that my diverse portfolio of business interests thrive and prosper.

But when one reaches my age, a certain weariness with all of this can slowly overtake one, so the prospect of launching a completely new hotels venture, and seeing it succeed would indeed be a refreshing diversion, so you do have my permission to speak to my daughter," he said, signalling that this interview was at an end.

Brad said 'goodnight' and made his way elatedly back down the grand staircase to find Gabriella waiting in the hallway.

"How was your meeting?" she said, locking a slender arm through his and gently propelling him towards a side corridor, partly hidden by an elaborate Japanese printed screen, which he'd not noticed before. The sudden small physical contact again took him by surprise, but as he'd now had more than his normal intake of alcohol, topped up by Edelmira's generous nightcap, he took it as a friendly gesture.

"Rather well I'd say," he replied, as with a sudden deft movement, he found himself being pushed sideways and into an empty guest bedroom! No sooner had the door closed behind them, then Francesca, who was as tall as

Brad, pinned him back against it, wrapped her arms around him and kissed him full on the mouth. This was definitely not a good idea having only a few minutes earlier been given Edelmira's blessing to continue his fledgling romance his daughter. But the sweet scent of her probing body locked against his and the forced invasion of her tongue into his mouth, rapidly overwhelmed his weakening defences and he wrapped his arms around her sleek black dressed form. Now fully aroused and no longer in control, he pushed her, suddenly yielding and compliant body backwards and down onto the large double bed.

Twenty minutes later, their passion spent, Francesca calmly slid off her side of the bed, retrieved her scattered garments and retreated into the bathroom. "This will be our secret," she promised after she'd emerged and bid him follow her out in a couple of minutes and make his way back to his apartment.

Chapter 18

After a short official courtship and a low-key wedding at The Hacienda Jimarenal, Brad and Francesca honeymooned in the Greek islands because both had solo memories of time spent relaxing on deserted beaches, while eating grilled fish and salads with fetta and olives, and had later flown to the Spanish Costas, where fledgling tourism developments were just taking off. They'd intended honeymooning for six weeks, but were on their way back home, after four, burning with a fevered ambition for the furthering of their hotel chain plans.

Francesca had called her father from Barcelona where they'd spent a couple of days making useful contacts before flying home via the United States, only to discover he was back on the small family estate on the Pacific coast of Costa Rica.

It took a week to get home and both were tired and drained from all the travelling by the time their light aircraft landed on the grass strip amidst the trees and they'd been collected by jeep and driven for some miles along a dirt road towards a small plateau overlooking the ocean. It was Brad's first visit and although Francesca had told him all about her father's estate, it surpassed all his expectations as the perfect place for a man of substance to retreat from the world, relax and unwind. Their guest suite in the large colonial style house, clearly built by a wealthy individual in much earlier days, overlooked the canopy, because the building was right on the edge of a plateau and level with tops of most of the surrounding trees.

"This is magnificent," Brad called out from the balcony and back into the room where Francesca had already unpacked and was walking naked into the shower, her jet black hair flowing freely behind her. It was around 7pm when they finally made their way along the corridor and down a wide staircase into a small central courtyard, where an ornate fountain sent a splatter of water into a small raised pool.

Brad was now beginning to take in and appreciate his surroundings, glancing up at the high glass canopy enclosing the courtyard, as Francesca led the way into a large kitchen come dining room. "Ah, there you are," a vaguely familiar and welcoming voice called out.

Walking casually towards them, in the same slinky back number she'd been wearing on that fateful evening back at the Hacienda Jimarenal, was Gabriella, wine glass in hand and looking as stunning as ever.

"Have you had a wonderful time?" she asked, looking directly and knowingly at Brad, as Edelmira entered the room and she turned to greet him. "Our wanderers have returned so let me fix you a cocktail before we sit down to eat," she invited.

And what would you both like?" She asked, slipping behind a small bar made of highly polished exotic woods.

Brad was momentarily thrown completely off his balance. Here was the woman, who'd had her way with him just a few months earlier, sitting naked astride his upturned form. Now here she was acting as hostess in a scene that needed no further explanation in that she was clearly his father-in-law's mistress.

Edelmira, sitting next to Gabriella, listened intently and without interruption as Francesca and his new son-in-law set out their thinking after they'd finished supper. No, they told him, if this new hotel chain was going to have the best chance of success, it should not be launched on their doorstep in the Caribbean, but all along Spain's still mostly unspoilt Mediterranean coast with its chain of long sandy beaches and with direct flight access to the huge European market.

"And not only Spain Edelmira," said Brad, taking over from Francesca. "There's also the southern coast of

Portugal and practically all of the Greek islands, all ripe for tourism," he pointed out.

"I think that's enough business talk for now," said Gabriella and Edelmira agreed, but as he and Francesca were about to return to their apartment, he invited Brad to join him for a nightcap. "You are going to need far more funds to satisfy your rapidly expanding aspirations than can be raised as security on your family real estate," he pointed out. They were now sitting together in two wicker chairs, close to the splashing fountain in the courtyard. "Oh! and by the way, the deeds for which, are now in my possession," Edelmira said, looking straight at Brad to see how his son-in-law would react. "That's a relief then, so I assume we do have enough funds to, at least, make a start," Brad replied, giving no hint that he'd been in the least bit phased by the news.

In a few of his quieter and innermost moments, he'd rationalised that all he was really doing was borrowing on his birthright, a debt he would repay one day, if the circumstances ever required him to do so. But what Edelmira did not tell him, nor was ever likely to, was that while the Toronto business was being 'taken care of,' one Harry Jacobs had gone missing and was later found drowned on the lake shore. It was the necessary tying up of a loose end which linked his son-in-law to the

Jimarenal Corporation, because if such ends were not dealt with, they could one day begin to unravel.

Brad and Francesca did not surface until mid-morning and joined Edelmira for a brunch on his veranda, because Gabriella had gone off with a wildlife guide and fisherman to see if they could find a whale and her calf, which had been spotted out in the gulf.

"Now my children, you must step back from your enthusiasm for a moment and take a longer view of your hotel plans," Edelmira told them after they had finished eating and had been served coffee. It was clearly a form of endearment he'd never used before and in that moment neither Brad nor Francesca knew quiet how to take it. They were gratified that it demonstrated his great fondness for them both, but it also suggested they were not old enough to know their own minds and that he was now the one in their driving seat.

"Go on Papa. Do share your thoughts," Francesca said, brushing aside any negative feelings she might have had.

"What you have suggested sounds an excellent prospect, so now you must go back and acquire all the prime locations you require, not for just one hotel, but for twenty or even more, not only in Spain, but as you have suggested, in Portugal and the Greek islands as well, because the longer you leave it, the more expensive and difficult to find they will become," he advised.

"But Papa that will be an enormous task and will cost a huge sum," Francesca pointed out. "Yes, but the corporation has the cash and the right people to assist in making the most of this golden opportunity."

What he did not tell them, was that he'd already reached the conclusion it was time the corporation transferred part of its operations out of the Americas. Business in the region was becoming ever more difficult to conduct, what with Castro now in power in Cuba, factional guerrilla operations all over the place, constant meddling by the CIA and those they funded into positions of influence often reneging on their agreements.

Brad hesitated for a moment before speaking in an effort to scramble his thoughts together at the prospect of such a huge enterprise. "You are right Edelmira. The time to strike is indeed right now before too many other players get onto the field, but what part will there be for Francesca and I to play if the corporation becomes totally involved" he asked. "That's easy to answer. You are both enthusiastic and highly intelligent young people and I do not mean that in any condescending way. You are the future of this family and this is your project, so you will have total control over its direction. Putting it simply, I believe you should return to Spain as soon as you are rested and start identifying all your preferred sites. Antonio or Lucas will follow shortly and set up an office in Barcelona from which they'll put together an acquisition team to act on your instructions," he told them.

"Papa that's brilliant," said Francesca, now looking at Brad for his support. They returned to their suite on a high, fell onto the bed consumed by a cocktail of passion and adrenalin and made their first child.

Chapter 19

With Brad and Francesca's determination to build their own empire backed by the seemingly endless resources, and sometimes malign influence of the corporation, The Grand Hotel Edelmondo chain grew remarkably quickly. Deals were done with airlines to fly thousands of the newly affluent young holidaymakers from all over the UK and Europe to the Spanish Costas, as well as to Portugal's Algarve coast and to the larger of the Greek islands.

Brad Junior's arrival, followed two years later by his brother Frankie, did little to interrupt the speed of progress.

All along, Francesca, like Brad, was able to rationalise and gloss over the inescapable fact that the funds, which fuelled their legitimate hotel business, were mostly illegally gained through protection, blackmail and deception, and that half the diverse range of companies within the Jimarenal Corporation were actually fronts for a huge drug money laundering operation.

Such was the complexity of these nefarious enterprises, spread as they were across a number of countries in central and South America, that investigating officers from external agencies, who were occasionally alerted, found it extremely difficult to figure out which enterprises were legitimate and which were not and walked away. After all, what was the point in opening such cans of worms especially when it was realised that people of importance and influence could be involved? It was reasoned.

Francesca's complicity was explained by the fact that following her mother's early death from cancer, Edelmira kept her close to him and she'd grown up surrounded by his close confidants who became genuinely fond of their 'Little Princes.' She was an extremely bright child, who as she grew older, naturally became attuned to the business environment around her and to accepting that which might have appeared in some ways dubious, to be simply the way that her Papa did things.

Being home educated and in the company of adults almost all the time, it would have been difficult for her to have any other moral compass against which to make a judgement.

Both Brad Junior, and his younger brother Frankie, were raised, speaking Spanish and English on Edelmira's Costa Rican estate, which Brad and Francesca made their family base when not operating out of the Barcelona offices, now the hub of the corporation's European operations.

Edelmira, accompanied by Gabriella, acting ostensibly as his personal assistant, moved regularly both in and out of their lives, attending board meetings back at the Villa Maria and in Barcelona. She never again tried it on with Brad, but as the years progressed, their once passionate love making, developed into a shared, but unspoken intimacy, succoured by the occasional knowing look across the meeting room or the dinner table, if he and Francesca happened to be dining with Edelmira in some fashionable restaurant or back home in Costa Rica.   Francesca was nobody's fool and gradually grew to understand there was something more than simple close family friendship shared between her husband and her father's younger lover.

This made her feel excluded and slowly eroded her love for Brad and the closeness she once shared with him. Francesca had always shied away from conflict ever since she was a child and the idea of tackling Brad about an issue that was little more than a growing conviction, was a complete anathema to her, and especially because of what it might do to her beloved Papa.

But by the time of their latest site prospecting trip to Goa, and the first they'd shared with their sons, was coming to a close, she'd pretty much made up her mind it was time to start distancing herself from her husband, but only in a very gradual way.

"Do we really need to go on doing all of this for the rest of our lives?" Francesca asked on the final night before their departure. Brad Junior and Frankie were both asleep in an adjoining hotel room, while they enjoyed a quiet drink on their balcony before getting down to all the packing. "We don't have anything left to prove anymore and we've surely amassed enough of a personal fortune not to have to work for another single day if we choose not to." The question caught Brad by surprise. "But what would you want to do instead?" he asked. "I don't quite know yet, but possibly something creative, while donating more of my time to the boys, while you carry on growing the business, if that is what you want to do. Papa is spending more time back home in Costa Rica these days and I know he'd appreciate seeing more of me. Come to think of it, he's had far more quality time with our children lately than we have."

Brad knew better than to try and discourage Francesca once she'd made up her mind about something, but he also knew he was nowhere near ready to throw in the towel in favour of a much quieter life.

In the end a compromise was reached with Brad handing over control of the European and new India business to a trusted friend and colleague, who'd been introduced by Edelmira and transferred over from the Jimarenal Corporation to the European hotel group some four years earlier. This left Brad free to return to their original concept of developing the hotel business much closer to home on Costa Rica's Caribbean coast while being able to spend more time with Francesca and their sons.

Frankie was quite artistic, taking after his mother, while Brad Junior started showing interest in becoming involved in either the corporation or the hotel group, as the years sped by.

But things never worked out as planned because the business friend and colleague soon decided that Europe was not for him and resigned, forcing Brad to fly to Barcelona far more often than was ever envisaged. True the flight links had improved incredibly since those heady early days, but it still meant he was away from the family estate on the Pacific coast far more than he was there.

Francesca never seemed to mind and when finally, their sons disappeared off to university in Panama and went to live in the apartment, where she and Brad had their first evening together, she actually relished her now almost total freedom.

Edelmira had become increasingly frail over recent years with Brad and Gabriella now deputising for him and co-hosting important meetings back at the hacienda headquarters in Bogota. She was still an extremely attractive woman and sharp as a razor, who had now been close to the leaver of power at the top of the corporation for many years.

Brad's decision to concentrate on Edelmondo Hotel Group developments closer to home was not without its challenges because there were competitors in the field. He had set his heart on acquiring one particular site with considerable potential, but so had another hotel developer, who'd already amassed a considerable holding in the region. Strangely their paths had never crossed, but now they'd agreed to meet at a beach hotel and golf complex in the Dominican Republic, conveniently owned and operated by a third party, to see if something could be sorted out.

Chapter 20

Hugo Andrews and his personal assistant, Charlie Potter, were the first to arrive and settled in adjoining rooms because, while she certainly enjoyed having sex with her boss,' she also insisted on having her own space.

Hugo had come to see Charlie as his confidant in the three years since he'd first met her and, more recently, as a second marriage prospect and new mother for his seven-year-old son James. Charlie, he learned early on in their relationship, had spent virtually all her working life in the UK hotels industry, starting out as a front of house receptionist at a four-star property in Bristol, and steadily working her way up to become General Manager. From there, she had gone on to take a number of higher profile positions in larger and more prestigious properties.

She'd been flown out to the Caribbean by her then employer's hotel group to assist with the opening of a new shoreside golf hotel and country club. Their paths had first crossed when Hugo decided to hold a meeting there with a party of close friends and associates to check out the opposition and to try out the new course. It was Charlie who'd given him the obligatory show around and he'd found her instantly attractive and extremely enthusiastic. He left it a couple of weeks before inviting her out for dinner and then when, during the course of the evening, she happened to mention that her job was now done and she'd soon be flying back to the UK, he invited her to join his company as his personal assistant and before the evening was over, she'd accepted.

Now he was about to propose, despite the one fly in the ointment, namely his equally strong-willed mother, who'd taken a more or less instant dislike to Charlie from the day her son had invited her over for lunch. It hadn't taken her many minutes to see that her beloved Hugo was more than a little attracted to this youngish and clearly strong-willed woman, who would certainly be a rival when it came to her son's, and more importantly, her grandson's affections, if they should marry.

Hugo's first thought was to propose that evening over dinner, but then decided he'd rather wait until the forthcoming meeting was over. He was a shrewd and fast thinking operator with a determined drive to succeed at whatever challenge he set himself, which was why his Caribbean hotels operation had become so successful. But he was also scrupulously honest in all his dealings and that quality he'd learned through a quiet word here

and there, did not apply to the shadowy Jimarenal
Corporation, owners of the Edelmondo Group.
In short, Hugo was not particularly looking forward to this
face-to-face meeting with Chief Executive Brad Moreton,
who on Edelmira's advice, had changed his name from
Meyer at the beginning of their business association.
This was deliberately to muddy the waters when it came
to any links with his dubious past professional life back
home in Toronto, and more importantly, from Edelmira's
private perspective, the elimination of Harry Jacobs.
Hugo had booked a small ground floor conference room
because it was the one closest to the hotel's helipad for
the Edelmondo Group people, due to fly in at 11am.
It had a balcony overlooking the golf course where he
and Charlie waited for their guests to arrive. They heard
the small Sikorski, but did not see it coming because it
flew in over the hotel and hovered momentarily, like a
demented bee, before descending onto the pad. To
Hugo's surprise, two figures, a man and a woman,
climbed out of the machine and began hurrying towards
them, briefcases in hand. "This should be interesting,"
Hugo muttered, half to himself and half to Charlie.
Brad Moreton was slim and good looking and probably
about his own age, as was his smartly dressed woman
companion, he noted. The four broke the ice with small

talk while being served refreshments by a white gloved young woman from a mobile station at the back of the room. But they got straight down to business, sitting opposite each other at a boardroom table, the minute the trolly had been wheeled away and the door had closed quietly behind them.

It quickly became clear to Charlie that while Hugo's rival was leading their side of the discussion, the Gabriella woman was his equal and the more subtly confrontational of the two. Yet it had become pretty self-evident to her from the start, that both Hugo and this business rival really got on, although there was something vaguely familiar about him, she thought for just a single fleeting moment.

As it turned out, the meeting ended completely amicably with Brad agreeing to withdraw his group's interest in the property in exchange for Hugo's agreement not to pursue another prospect, they'd quickly discovered, they were both tentatively looking at.

"I think you must be going a little soft Brad," Gabriella called out, half in jest, as the Sikorski lifted off and they waved at Hugo and Charlie, who'd braved it as close to the helipad as they could, to see their guests off. "No, because I think the other property has far more potential," Brad shouted back.

That evening, Hugo did propose to Charlie, who happily agreed to become Mrs Charlotte Andrews!

Brad later picked up the phone to Francesca, whose calls to him had gradually become more infrequent as his busy weeks had flown by. He knew he hadn't been paying either her or the boys much attention of late, but there again, it was a two-way street and they'd not been overly fussed about talking to him.

It seemed entirely natural that should be the case, because their sons were now busy making their way in the world. He couldn't remember being overly fussed about speaking to his parents once he left home. They'd be back in touch when they wanted or needed something, had been his rationale.

That had certainly been the case a year earlier when Brad Junior had turned up with his then fiancé and now wife, seeking some funding for a smart restaurant they wanted to open in Los Angeles, where she had grown up as a member of a family of established restaurateurs. Edelmira had earlier taken a shine to his grandson's partner and could understand why they wanted their independence rather than going to her family for financial support.

"After all that's exactly what you and Francesca wanted," he'd reminded Brad, who'd become adverse over the years to shelling out funds, unless it was really necessary, a view he shared with Gabriella.

Edelmira's relationship with his beloved daughter had become just a little strained as the years went by, because she was not comfortable about having Gabriella as her proxy stepmother. Then there was Brad, whom he'd regarded as the son he'd never had and who got on extremely well with Gabriella.

While Brad Junior and his wife were well ensconced in their successful restaurant enterprise in Los Angeles, Frankie had set himself up as an artist working out of a studio in Boston. Brad knew Francesca was funding him, which was perfectly all right, because she had substantial funds of her own provided by her father.

Francesca was now spending quite a lot of her time with her son and had even started painting herself, and was in business mode when she called Brad, currently back on the Costa Rican estate with Edelmira and Gabriella.

"Querida, I think it's time we had a legal separation and a divorce after a year, unless anything changes," she announced.

She'd always called him 'darling' in Spanish and saw no reason to change. She still had a good deal of affection for him after all the years they'd spent together, although she no longer loved him, and that being the case, had no desire to spend the rest of her life with him. Brad had tacitly accepted, as time went by that, they had fallen out of love with one another, but was still taken by surprise by her out of the blue proposal.

"Don't you think you should come home, so that we can at least discuss this face-to- face?" he countered, although he was not at all sure he actually wanted to see her. "No, I can't see any sence in that, but I'm going to ask Papa to fly over and spend a little quality time with me in the Panama City apartment, preferably without Gabriella on this occasion," she added, pointedly.

Edelmira did respect his daughter's wishes and flew back to Panama City a week later to help her start drawing up a separation plan, which would eventually lead to the dividing up of the substantial funds they held in common.

Edelmira was unhappy that is daughter wanted a separation because he could not see why things should not go on as they were, but if that was what she wanted, then he would not stand in her way.

The divorce eventually came and was amicably concluded with Francesca agreeing to accept twenty million US dollars to sever all connection with the Jimarenal Corporation. This was really only a token of what she was due, but it was worth it because by now she'd met a good honest man and had no desire to have anything more to do with the shady organisation.

In her heart of hearts, she'd rather not have taken a single laundered dollar, but she'd grown up and spent her entire life living on the trappings of wealth the organisation had provided, and knew she could not contemplate poverty in any of its degrading forms, or being financially dependent on others. Looking back, she'd deeply regretted that she and Brad had not insisted on keeping their fledgling hotels group a completely clean operation and had not succumbed to her father's willing offer of assistance, once they'd used up all Brad's funds.

Still what good were regrets? So now she would do all she could to stay clear of Brad and Gabriella and encourage her sons to do the same, when it came to accepting tempting offers of financial support for any future project, or business opportunity that might come their way.

That was an insurance policy, because if one day the Jimarenal Corporation fell apart, as inevitably she felt it would, and all its many corrupt dealings were exposed to the investigative light of day, then having her boys drawn into the financial mire, was the very last thing she wanted. But sadly, for one of her sons, the temptations of wealth and power were going to be impossible to resist.

Chapter 21

It was just another sultry sunny morning. A family of howler monkeys were feeding and moving about in the canopy beyond the villa and a large Iguana was clamped to his usual trunk, when Gabriella entered Edelmira's room. She saw at once that he was sitting in his normal chair on the balcony overlooking the treetops and the ocean. But something wasn't right. His bed hadn't been slept in and he appeared to be slumped in his chair. "Edel," she said, as she hurried towards him. The old man was dead and it looked as if he'd been out there all night.

"Brad where are you?" she called, hurrying out onto the covered landing and peering down into the central courtyard.

Later that morning, when the old man's body had been removed, and before he called to break the news to Francesca and his sons, Brad, accompanied by Gabriella, went back into his room and removed his safe keys from the place his father-in-law had told him they'd be in case he became incapacitated, or died.

The strong box was behind an easily detachable panel in Edelmira's adjoining study, and when he swung open its heavy steel door and looked down, a large and bulky vanilla envelope with his name on was lying face up in front of him.

Lifting it out, he carried it to Edelmira's desk, and sat down to open it with Gabriella standing and looking over his shoulder.

Reaching in, he carefully drew out its contents, comprising of a letter and another smaller and much older package tied with red ribbon.

Heart beginning to thump, he opened the envelope with the antique silver paper knife, that had lain on the desk for years, and unfolded the letter.

'My dear Brad. I am sure you've known that I have always looked upon you as the son I never had and you have not disappointed me,' he read. 'In the enclosed packet you will find the deeds to your father and uncle's Toronto real estate, which you assumed were used as the collateral for the launching of your now very successful Edelmondo Hotels Group.

But that was not the case because, in the end, you and Francesca were funded entirely by the corporation and those deeds have remained in this safe ever since. You might well ask, why that was so and the reason is, that once you and Francesca married and you were my son-in-law, and your family were now my extended family, I had no desire for you to take and use the deeds, which I extracted from your father and uncle by coercion. Your family were simply told that unless they sent us the deeds in exchange for the long lease, then they'd never see you again. You never questioned me as to how the deeds were obtained, so I never told you. As this is the time for confessions, I must now also tell you that the copy of my last will and testament, which you will also find in the drawer at the bottom of the safe, has now been superseded by one which I wrote on my last visit to Francesca and is held by my lawyers in Panama City. It can be read after a short memorial service, which must be held there in the coming weeks, by which time you will have had my remains buried close to my favourite garden seat overlooking the ocean.

The reason for this is simple in that I have no desire for any of our associates, who may wish to show their respects, coming out here and invading my privacy even though I am no more.'

Brad sat back in his father-in-law's desk chair and gazed out of the half open window as he tried to come to terms, with what he had just read. "Aren't you going to open the other packet to see if those deeds are in there, Brad?"

He shook his head, suddenly not wishing to have anything more to do with the deceit he had perpetrated on his father and uncle all those years ago.   "No, if

Edel says they're in there, then they're in there," he replied. "But far more importantly, what's in his new will? I think it's time I broke the news to Francesca and the boys," he said reaching for the telephone.

"I'll leave you to do that then," said Gabriella, turning and walking slowly and thoughtfully out of the room. Everything now seemed to be uncertain and she did not like uncertainty. Before his death, it had generally been agreed in various dinner table conversations, when the subject of succession had come up, that Brad would take over as the corporation's new Chairman and Managing Director with her as his de facto, second in command of its largest division, the other two smaller ones already being headed up by Antonio and Lucas's sons Juan and Jose, who'd both come into the organisation some years earlier and were proving able, highly aggressive and effective operators. But what could Edel have done that might now throw all the playing cards back up into the air? she wondered.

Some sixty of the corporation's close associates from around South and Central America, the Caribbean and Europe flew in to Panama City for the memorial service. Chief among them, and long regarded more as 'family' were Antonio and Lucas, now both in their late seventies.

Their sons Juan and Jose, were accompanied by a cadre of politicians and others feeling it necessary to show their respects, or seen to be doing so. The service was short and almost business like with little pomp and ceremony, which Edelmira would have appreciated, and there was only one short eulogy given by Brad Junior, who sat in the front row with Brad and Francesca and his brother Frankie. Their partners occupied the row behind, along with Gabriella, Antonio and Lucas and their sons. It had surprised Gabriella that Brad had not delivered the tribute from the lectern, but as his son spoke quietly, and authoritatively, about his much-loved grandfather, his zest for life and his many achievements, it suddenly dawned on her, that Brad Junior might soon be taking a far more prominent role in the family's business affairs than anyone had anticipated.

Gabriella was an extremely perceptive woman, one of the many attributes that had enabled her to work her way into such a prominent position at the top of the corporation, and the very thought that, that just might be the way the wind was now blowing, was worrying, to say the least. There could be no love lost between her and Brad Junior, who would naturally, only see her as the woman, who'd eventually undermined his mother's love for his father, while at the same time worming her way into his grandfather's affections.

There had been the traditional reception in a smart restaurant conveniently close by so that those who wished could walk there in the lunchtime sunshine, but by 3pm, everyone, except the immediate family and close friends, had offered their final condolences, made their excuses and had left.

As the numbers dwindled, and the opportunities for avoiding Francesca became more difficult, Gabriella claimed a headache, drove to the airport and caught a late afternoon flight back to Bogota and then took a taxi back to the hacienda.

As the car approached the almost stately colonial style building, she found herself remembering the day, all those years ago, when she'd first made that now, oh so familiar journey, to be interviewed for the receptionist's job.   She went straight to her apartment to rest and to await the phone call that she knew would inevitably come from Brad, once the will had been read. She fixed herself a drink, while the bath was running, stripped off and climbed in for a much-needed soak.

Thinking back on the reception and the way Brad Junior had stayed close to his father over the lunchtime and how she'd heard his proud mother-in-law saying how well the couple's restaurant business was doing, only seemed to confirm her suspicions, that a change was coming. Frankie, she'd noticed, had stayed close to Francesca, and had been cold towards her when she'd approached to make her condolences. But what had really confirmed her fears was the inescapable fact that Brad, her confidant for all these years, had also practically disowned her during the gathering.

It was as if he'd actually known all along, or had since been told, the contents of his father-in-law's will!

The call came just after 9pm. She was relieved that Brad sounded very much his familiar self, albeit tired from all the proceedings of the day, and actually apologised for practically ignoring her during the reception.

He had, she accepted, been in an embarrassingly difficult position with her being on one side and his ex-wife and sons on the other. So might she have completely miss read the situation all along? Her hopes rose. "So what were the changes in the will?" she asked. There followed a long pause as if Brad was delaying the news to the final second. She could practically hear him drawing in a deep breath.

"Edel has instructed that in order to firmly secure the future stability of the corporation, that Brad Junior should be offered the role of Deputy Chairman and Chief Executive and he's accepted. It seems Edel had become very impressed by the way Brad and Alexandra were making such a success of their business and that it was actually Brad who tentatively suggested taking some active interest in the corporation.

"How do you feel about that then?" she asked quietly. There was another pause as if he too was now considering how best to answer the question.

"Well actually I'm delighted at the prospect of having Brad by my side, because it will give me the perfect excuse not to have to further promote Antonio and Lucas's boys, who've both been quietly pressing for a more central role, urged on by their father's, I suspect. But Brad gets on really well with them and working together, they could easily become the future of our organisation, once I retire," he said.

Now Gabriella could not contain her hurt and her fears a moment longer. "But Brad you must realise this change puts me in the most awkward position, because it's been made pretty clear that neither of your sons care much for me for all the reasons I certainly don't need to go in to." As she spoke, Gabriella was seeing with crystal clarity that as long as Edel was alive, her position within the organisation was rock solid. But now that he was gone, she was on shifting sands and that there was really no way out for her, other than to walk away with the considerable fortune she quietly amassed over the years. The fact that Brad was now so keenly in favour of his son coming into the corporation, only strengthened her view that it was finally time for her to go.

Within twenty-four hours she'd packed her bags, handed in the keys to her apartment at reception and left by taxi for the airport. She'd become close friends with a number of her work colleagues at the hacienda over the years, some of the outside staff being, old stagers, whom she'd known since her early days. But she felt too humiliated to say goodbye because of the questions it would have raised. The last person she saw as her taxi swept out of the hacienda and down the long winding drive towards the banana plantation, was Manny, who was in charge of the greenhouses and supplied her with all the fresh table flowers she'd needed for the many receptions she'd organised over the years.

Chapter 22

As Brad had hoped, his son and daughter-in-law moved easily and seamlessly into life at the hacienda, having put a trusted friend and associate in charge of their restaurant operation.

Gabriella's sudden departure had come as a surprise, but also a relief to Brad, who'd foreseen all sorts of tensions arising had she remained. True they'd never become secret lovers following that first evening at the hacienda and it was shortly afterwards that she'd become Edelmira's mistress. But they had been close and he knew it was that closeness that had finally driven the wedge between him and Francesca. But with Gabriella now permanently off the scene, Francesca was no longer averse to making the occasional flying visit to the hacienda, or to the Costa Rican estate, bringing Frankie and his wife and daughter with her, for a family birthday or some other celebration, which reminded him very much of earlier and happier times.

As Brad had predicted, his son, now working closely with Juan and Jose, formed an easy triumvirate that began slowly expanding the Jimarenal Corporation's dubious and unsavoury activities, while still using their considerable resources to support up and coming politicians and others in high places. As Edel himself had pointed out many years earlier, the people they supported were like so many coffee beans planted and nurtured, so that once they'd grown to maturity, they could yield a rich crop of government contracts and other favours needed to further the corporation's interests in the mining, civil and private property development, tourism and the gaming industry sectors. It had slightly surprised Brad that his eldest boy had so easily slipped into the corporation's dubious ways of doing business, but there again, maybe it was the old adage 'like father, like son.' Brad finally stepped back from taking an active role in the corporation's affairs and following in Edelmira's footsteps, retreated to the family estate.

Brad Junior and Frankie, who'd both fathered a son and daughter, flew out for the occasional family holidays, which was a source of great comfort to him following their mother's completely unexpected death from a stroke some two years earlier.

But then one day towards the end of January, Brad received a late evening call from his son, saying something had come up which he did not wish to discuss on the telephone, so he'd be making a flying visit the following afternoon.

Brad was sitting out on the veranda overlooking the top of the canopy and towards the Pacific Ocean in the same favourite chair that his father-in-law had occupied for so many years, when he heard the light aircraft flying over. It somehow gave him a sense of destiny that he was following in Edel's footsteps and was, himself, now the wise senior counsellor, to be consulted from time to time. But for his son to be coming to see him on one specific matter was unheard of and meant it must be of considerable importance. Half an hour later, Brad Junior came out onto the balcony and they embraced before he settled himself into one of the two other comfortable wicker chairs, so often occupied in the past by Edel's close associates Antonio and Lucas, who had now also passed away.

"Now what's this all about my son," he said, not looking at him, but gazing straight out over the ocean, as Edel had done so many times before him. "Word has come that there is a Toronto businessman making enquiries about the corporation and especially about your whereabouts and that he can be expected to fly into San Jose shortly." Brad Junior could see instantly his news had certainly shocked his father, who now turned to him, ashen faced at suddenly being confronted by the past he'd so conveniently buried. "Oh! my son. There is something about my early life you now need to know and when I have told you, I think you will understand why I have kept it a secret from you and your brother all these years."

Sitting close, Brad Junior listened in silence as the story of his father's deceit and all the circumstances surrounding it, slowly unfolded. When at last he'd finished, he reached across, and taking the old man's hand, gently squeezed it in an unspoken act of understanding and solidarity. "So what is that we should do, or that you would have me do now Papa?"

Brad settled back in his chair and returned his gaze to the ocean as he carefully and methodically went through all the options.

"Deeds tend to stay locked away and pretty much forgotten until such time that a property is to change hands and then, of course, their whereabouts suddenly becomes of great importance," he said slowly, spilling out the words as the thoughts entered his head. "The same is true of long leases, so have our friends in San Jose let us know as soon as this businessman arrives and, if possible, what it is that he's seeking and then we can decide what needs to be done my son," said Brad. "Now before you go, because I'm assuming you don't have the time to stay over, you must tell me what my grandchildren are up to at the moment."

Brad was still sitting out on the balcony as the light aircraft again flew overhead, but his mind was now so full of memories of his early life that the noise barely registered. Why had he simply rubbed his past out, rather than making some effort at a reconciliation, once he was wealthy and could have returned like the Prodigal Son? he asked himself. No, he'd never wanted to go back because, although it had been so easy with the impetuousness of youth to rationalise what he had done, he was too deeply ashamed and he doubted that his deceit and all the anxiety and hurt it had caused his family would ever have been forgiven. Then Brad was remembering the fishing trips up to the family's lakeside camp and how on those rare occasions he'd actually enjoyed his 'father's' company and then his thoughts switched to that last business trip over to the UK and how he'd met that attractive young woman guide, whom he'd suddenly invited over to stay. The happy, sunny day he'd spent with her was still writ large in his memory, even after all these years.

On an impulse, they'd popped into a small jewellery shop, near the city's famous Clifton Suspension Bridge and he'd insisted on buying her a silver St Christopher as a keepsake, despite her protestations. And then he was recalling his arrival back in Toronto and that fateful call from Harry Jacobs that had changed the entire course of his life. "Good evening, sir, I'm sorry to disturb you, but are you coming down for dinner or would you like something out here or in your room?" a familiar voice enquired.

"No, Laurence, I won't come down again this evening, so maybe bring me up a tray with some cold meats, bread and a little fruit."

Laurence was a sort of maitre d, but in his case not for a restaurant, but for the general smooth running of the villa, being in charge of the dozen or so catering, housekeeping, maintenance and gardening staff, who kept the house and its extensive gardens and grounds in smooth running order.

He was the son of an itinerant Frenchman, who'd somehow found his way to the Gulf of Ossa and married a local girl.

Laurence had come to help out at the villa as a young man and had never left. He was bright and might have gone far in the wider world, but he liked being at the villa. The pay was generous by local standards and he needed the cash to help support his parents, who had fallen on hard times. Edelmira realised Lawrence's talents long before he retired and put him in overall charge, a decision he never regretted.

It was ten days later that Brad Junior returned with the news that it was one Jonathan Meyer, senior partner with Toronto lawyers Joseph B Meyer, accompanied by a British woman, Miss Corine Potter, who'd checked in to the exclusive Alhambra Hotel in San Jose and were actively seeking both him and the return of the deeds to the Toronto real estate. "This is more than likely to be my uncle Joe's grandson," said Brad. "So, what do you want me to do then Papa?" asked his son, as they were again sitting and looking out over the ocean. "My inclination is to have a courier hand over the deeds and bid them return from whence they came," he replied. "But then again, it would be interesting to invite them here and I think I might be warming to that idea my son. "Ah, therein lies a small difficulty, because they found their way to us through Agrimenta Investments. We've been keeping them at arm's length for some time since learning they were being targeted by Costa Rica's serious crime agency. So it's possible the authorities also know about Sen Meyer's arrival and could be tailing him and this woman. If they're still at The Alhambra, we'll assume the security people are on to them, although I think it's unlikely, and find a way of lifting them and bringing them here, but only if you're sure that's what you want because it will involve us in an element of risk", he warned. "Do we not have people in high places in San Jose, who might owe us a favour, should we need one?" he asked. "Yes, we do Papa, so I'll see what can be done," He knew quite well that once his father had made up his mind, then there was no dissuading him and besides, it could be interesting to have a window opened on his father's former life, always a closed book as far as he and his brother were concerned, up until now.

Chapter 23
Now

Georges was right. Looking down from the cabin windows of the light aircraft as it flew steadily along the jungle fringed Pacific coastline, at around twelve thousand feet, the view was spectacular, especially when they passed over the mouth of small rivers and could see the light brown, silty water, flooding out and staining the brilliant turquoise of the ocean.
Speaking just loud enough to hear one another over the drone of the aircraft's twin engines, Corinne and Jonathan came to the inevitable conclusion that her father was their abductor, because, why otherwise, were they being treated like VIP guests?
They'd only been flying for what seemed less than forty minutes, when the aircraft started losing height and flew in between the trees to land on a grassy runway.
Corinne spotted a woman wearing a bright red dress standing by a pram at the edge of the strip, waiting to cross over, and she somehow found that comforting.
When they came to a halt and the pilot had switched of the engine, Georges came past them to lean forward and open the cabin door and pull down the steps. "If you'd care to make your way over to the terminal, we'll

follow with your luggage," he instructed, pointing towards what was little more than a hut at the end of the runway. The humidity of the surrounding tropical forest enveloped them, like some unseen blanket the minute they left the comparative coolness of the aircraft. "I just can't get my head around this," Jonathan whispered. As they walked away from the aircraft, the white shirted pilot, still with his headphones on, gave them a friendly wave. "I feel like I'm in some weird nightmare," Corinne agreed, taking his hand.

"It's as if we're a couple of tourists on some exotic holiday of a lifetime, when the reality is that we've actually been hijacked and brought here against our will, when we should be boarding a flight to Denver," she said.

As they reached the terminal, they were passed by several people with suitcases walking towards the aircraft. For a moment, Corinne was tempted to waylay a rotund and friendly looking middle-aged man, in a lightweight white suit and Panama hat, and attempt to explain their plight. But a quick backward glance confirmed that their minders carrying the luggage had almost caught up with them.

"This way Sen Meyer," instructed Georges, who had now overtaken them and was leading the way out into a dirt carpark and towards what looked like a top of the range four-by-four.

"Would you take the rear seats please," he invited, as his sidekick went to the back of the vehicle to load the luggage.

"Look would you mind telling us just what the hell is going on here," Jonathan demanded. He was hovering by the now open door, on the point of refusing to climb in. "I've already told you Sen Meyer, that your travel plans have been changed for the next couple of days, but I can assure you that you will be back here shortly for your return flight to San Jose." Shrugging his shoulders, Jonathan climbed in, followed by Corinne, because there now seemed little point in any further protest.

The sun was lower in the sky and the shadows were lengthening as they drove along a reasonable paved road, close to the shore, before turning off on a dirt track, leading gradually upwards through the trees. At one point they stopped for a troop of howler monkeys and then their attention was grabbed by a couple of bright red parrot like birds. "Are they Macaws?" Corinne couldn't resist asking Georges. "That's right, they certainly are, but you'll be seeing lots of other wildlife while you are with us," he added, which was somehow a comforting thought.

Pulling up in front of a large set of elaborately patterned wrought iron gates, two men in light brown slacks with matching shirts appeared and opened them. Again, the fear they were now well and truly trapped and completely at the mercy of whomever had gone to such great lengths to get them there, gripped them. Before they had time to think on it any further, they were pulling up in front of a large colonial style house, surrounded by newer timber lodges, and Georges was already climbing out. As he did so, they spotted a slim casually dressed middle-aged man standing just a few paces away. Without further instruction, Jonathan and Corinne climbed out and stood there looking and feeling completely bewildered.

"Good evening, Sen Meyer and Senora Potter and welcome. My name is Laurence and I will be at your service during your stay. Your hosts are hoping you will join them for dinner around 7pm, but in the meantime, I will be showing you to your suite where hopefully you will have enough time to change and make yourselves comfortable." Feeling that any further protest or questions were now completely useless, they meekly followed Laurence towards the nearest lodge.

"I am sure you will find this to your liking, as most of our other guest do," he said, leading the way through a spacious lounge area and out onto a long wooden balcony with a magnificent view over the treetops, towards the ocean where the sun was almost setting. Laurence went through the motions of showing them where all the necessary facilities were before saying that when they were ready, they only had to dial seven on the bedside phone and he'd be over to collect them. "Oh, and by the way, should you wish to make a local or international call, it's triple seven." This last comment completely threw them. Was it deliberately made to put them at their ease, or set as a test? They could not tell. "I don't know about you, but I don't think I've ever been in such a surreal situation," said Jonathan coming forward and taking Corinne into his arms. "Guess we'd better make ourselves presentable then," she said after a few moments, gently pulling herself away and hefting her hurriedly packed case onto their mega king size bed and opening it.

They washed together and soaped one another in the beautifully tiled walk-in wet room in almost total silence, as if it was some pre ritual and then made themselves as presentable as they could for whatever was to follow.

"Are you ready then?" Jonathan asked. "As ready as I'll ever be," she replied, but then hesitated. "Wait a minute," she said, hurrying over to the suitcase, laying open on her side of the bed. After everything which had happened, she'd forgotten her mother's St Christopher to show to her father, but where was it? Somehow during the scrambled repacking for their hurried departure from The Alhambra in St Jose that morning, the little black box had disappeared.

"It's just got to be here," she muttered, delving more deeply into her jumbled suitcase, which she'd only partially unpacked, because she hoped theirs would be just a one-night stay.

At last, her burrowing fingers located it and she slipped into the leather clutch bag she'd packed just in case they went anywhere posh. 'What was that all about?' Jonathan wondered, but felt too distracted over what lay ahead, to question her as he picked up the bedside phone and dialled.

A few minutes later, Laurence was leading them though a side door and into a central courtyard filled with large exotic plants in heavy ornate terracotta pots and all covered by and impressive pagoda style conservatory roof. It was surprisingly cool after the heat of the day and there was an ornate central fountain splashing as they followed the maitre d' around it and into a large room opposite. It was lavishly furnished in the old colonial style with heavy wooden furniture and a highly polished wooden floor, a large circular dining table as its centre. Standing beside the table were two men who just had to be father and son.

"Sen Jonathan Meyer, Senora Potter, may I introduce you to Sen Brad Meyer and Sen Brad Meyer Junior. The sudden starkness of the introduction could not have been more surreal and totally threw both Jonathan and Corinne. It was if they were locked together in some weird drug fuelled dream!

'Can this really be happening? Can that elderly gentleman standing there and smiling at me really be my father?' Corinne asked herself. They must know Jonathan is related to them, but they won't have a clue who I am.

"My sincere apologies for Laurence's rather blunt introduction, but Papa and I could not see how else it was to be done," said Brad Junior, stepping forward and shaking hands, first with Brad, and then with Corinne before turning to his father.

"So you must be my Uncle Joe's grandson because the family likeness is remarkable," said Brad, stepping forward and embracing Jonathan. He'd intended a formal handshake, but to be so starkly confronted by his long-buried past had suddenly overwhelmed any formality. Seeing the old man was close to tears, Jonathan could do nothing else but reciprocate.

"I am pleased to meet you after so many years," he said, gently returning the embrace and resisting a strong urge to remonstrate with him over their abduction.

"So please now introduce us to your companion," said Brad turning to Corinne, who was almost rooted to the spot at seeing her father. She was tempted to say she was the daughter he'd condemned to early years of misery in and out of children's homes, because he had broken his promise to send an airline ticket for her then pregnant mother. But no, all that would have to wait until later. Instead, she told him she was Jonathan's partner from England and left it at that.

"You must both be hungry, if not a little tired after your unexpected journey here, so shall we sit down," Brad Junior invited, leading them to the dining table set with expensive silverware and fine crystal. They followed obediently, with Laurence suddenly materialising to draw out chairs for them and unfurl fine linen table napkins and place them on their laps.

'Could all the disturbing things they'd been told by those security people back in San Jose just a few short hours ago, which had sent them rushing back to the airport in a panic, really be true?' Jonathan was beginning to ask himself.

"Now Papa and I really do owe you our sincere apologies for the somewhat unorthodox way you were brought here when you should now really be back home in Toronto," said Brad Junior, as if he'd been reading his thoughts. "We assumed those completely misguided security people would be following you to the airport, so a little evasive action was required," he admitted.

"Yes, it was all rather unexpected to say the least," admitted Jonathan, glancing across at Corinne. He had been ready to launch into a tirade about what the hell they thought they were doing bringing them here against their will. But now he was intrigued to find out just how his great uncle had obtained the deeds to the family real estate, so recriminations could wait until later. There was also the question as to just when Corinne was going to reveal her true identity.

"Firstly, I hope you've realised by now that, although you were brought here in rather unusual circumstances, you are completely free to leave as soon as you like," Brad Junior assured them. "That can be tomorrow, or the day after, or even a little later if you prefer, because we are in a tropical paradise here and the Gulf of Ossa has some of the purest waters in the world and is teaming with wildlife," he told them. "But suffice is to say that when you are ready to depart, we'll fly you over the border into Panama City from where we'll book you first class tickets for Toronto, London, or anywhere else in the world you might wish to go," he promised.

"Forgive me for asking, but won't we need to return via San Jose to have our passports stamped to record we've left the country?" Jonathan asked. "Don't worry about that because it's a small formality," easily remedied," his cousin replied. "But while we are on formalities and before we settle down to do all our catching up together, perhaps we should dispense with the small matter that brought you here in the first place?" he suggested. With that, his father gave the smallest of signals to the maitre d, who was standing at a respectable distance and was at his side in an instant. "Laurence will you kindly bring me the large envelope you will find on my desk in the study and give it to Sen Meyer." Both he and Corinne watched, again struggling to believe what was actually happening, as the maitre d disappeared and a silence descended over the table. Then in what seemed like ages, but was only a couple of minutes, he returned and placed the envelope on the table in front of Jonathan. "Yes, it contains the deeds to our family real estate in Toronto, which were obtain for me after I left the city and made my life here in Central America," said Brad. "No doubt we can talk about that rather unfortunate chapter in my life, but right now may not be quite appropriate," he said quietly. Jonathan thanked him, suggesting that perhaps with the safe return of the deeds, that chapter could now be closed, unless he felt the need for explanations. "Spoken like the good man you clearly are," Brad responded.

"Bravo, so let's eat because I'm certainly feeling the need for sustenance," said Brad Junior, signalling for Laurence to hand around the menus, together with a wine list.

Sitting there so close to Jonathan and his most attractive companion, Brad was still struggling to come to terms with the fact that he'd found it so easy to cast aside his early life, never sparing a though for his 'father' or his long-suffering mother, or for all the grief and worry his disappearance must have caused them. Suddenly he wanted to know how the family, he'd so easily abandoned, had fared over all those lost years and now the person who could answer all those questions had come to seek him out and was sitting right there in front of him.

"So Jonathan, may I ask if your parents are still with us?" Brad asked quietly. "My mother still lives, but my father, Martin, died quite suddenly last fall, just after we'd returned from a trip to Europe and a visit to Britain," he revealed. "I am sorry to hear that," replied Brad. "Now Senora Potter. You're from England, so you must tell me how you came to meet Jonathan?" he asked. It was such an innocent question. Suddenly Corinne was the centre of all the attention and face began colouring with embarrassment. So had the wheel of fate turned full circle and was this the moment, she should reveal she was, in fact, his daughter and his son's half-sister? Now in her mind's eye, she was seeing and reliving the conversation she'd had with her mother, who after coming to stay as a guest at The Oreford Inn, had eventually revealed her true identity. Charlie had confided there'd come a moment when she'd almost decided it might have been better to have said nothing and to have returned to her retirement hotel in Sidmouth, comforted by the knowledge that her twins had found their way in the world and were both secure and happy. So should she now also reveal to this elderly stranger that she was his daughter, seeing the clearly dubious life both he and her half-brother had lived and were still living? They might have smoothed over and excused

themselves for the forceful way in which they'd abducted and brought them here against their will, but that did not make it right. Their abduction clearly proved that what those security people had said about the operations and malign influences of the shady corporation, which her father and half- brother controlled, was true!
Suddenly Corinne didn't want these people to know she was their own flesh and blood. To give them that knowledge would in some way be condoning all their actions and tainting her innocent family, she reasoned. Again, she thought of all the anguish her mother had suffered after being made pregnant by a man, who never sent for her and of the miserable time, she herself had spent in those children's homes. Suddenly, the tiny St Christopher, this stranger, because he was a stranger, had given her mother as a keepsake on that sunny day in Bristol all those years ago was also tainted, and she had no desire to show it to him to prove she was his daughter. No, it was all too much for her to even think about any more.

"I do hope you won't mind, but I'm suddenly not feeling at all well. It's probably the heat and all the excitement, so I think I'll go back to our room and lie down if you don't mind."

With her cheeks, now flushing bright red, and her heart beginning to pound, she got to her feet, as did everyone else. "I'll come back with you," said Jonathan, his voice full of concern. "No please stay. Laurence can see me back and I will be fine," she said giving him a weak smile.

Retracing her footsteps past the splashing fountain, she suddenly recalled, from seemingly out of nowhere, a snatch from a long conversation she'd had with Laura not long after they'd been reunited in Little Oreford. They'd realised that, as twins, they both suffered the same reaction when suddenly faced with a situation they could not handle. For Laura it had been a dinner party moment when guests had let slip that they were going to put in an offer to buy Albany House, which she wanted so desperately to be their family home!

Chapter 24

"Do you somehow feel you've laid a ghost to rest with the return of those deeds Papa?" Brad Junior asked. They were standing together on the balcony under a canopy of stars, after Jonathan had later excused himself and gone back to their suite.

"I think so my son, but it was also good for us both to hear from Jonathan a little more about the other life I left behind. They were quietly drinking Edelmira's favourite single malt whisky from the same tumblers he'd always used. "I know I've been reluctant to share my early life with you or your brother, but I guess I was both ashamed and felt a coward for simply allowing your grandfather to extract those deeds from my father and uncle under duress. And it grieves me now that I never spared a thought for all the anguish they must have suffered, especially my poor mother, who was the completely innocent party in all of this." Brad let out a long heart-felt sigh and took another sip of his whisky. "Look Papa. That was all a very long time ago, and besides, we have to admit to ourselves that we're not good people you and I," he said quietly. "No, you are right about that my son and, to tell you the truth, I'm quite relieved our guests have asked to leave tomorrow morning so will you see them off?" he asked.

"Don't worry Papa, I'll do that," he promised.

Both Corinne and Jonathan felt an overwhelming sense of relief the moment their light aircraft took off and swiftly climbed above the trees. She'd been asleep when he'd returned to their suite and there had been little time to talk in the morning due to their early departure.

Laurence had served them breakfast in the courtyard, where Brad Junior had come to say goodbye and to wish them a safe journey home.

"Well, I guess that's mission accomplished then, because you've got your deeds back and I've met my father and one of the two half-brothers I never knew I had," said Corinne. As she spoke, the twin engine private aircraft, now close to its optimum cruising height, banked over to the right enroute for Panama City.

"So you decided in the end that you wouldn't reveal who you were then," Jonathan, remarked. "Yes, I did," she replied, turning her head to gaze down from the cabin window, a clear signal that she didn't want to talk about it anymore.

From Panama City, they boarded an onward flight to Amsterdam's Schiphol hub and it was from here that Corinne called home to alert Bob to drive up in his

Bentley to collect her when she arrived at Heathrow. It was originally planned that Jonathan would accompany her back to Little Oreford for a further week, seeing their holiday had been cut so short.

But on the long flight from Panama, he decided it would be easier for him to pick up a connection from Amsterdam back to Toronto, and besides, he was now anxious to return his precious property deeds to the family vault as soon as possible. It had been agreed instead, that Corinne would fly out to join him for a long holiday in the spring, when the weather would be warmer, and which wasn't that far into the future anyway.

Corinne thought long and hard on the drive home, and during her first day back at The Oreford, about whether she should tell Charlie and her sister Laura that she'd actually met their father.

She finally decided it wouldn't be a good idea. After all, Laura had been against the whole idea of seeking him out in the first place and it was not as if it was a 'living happily ever after' story anyway. What benefit could there possibly be in her mother knowing that the father of her children was, putting it quite bluntly, the head of a criminal organisation, which had its evil tentacles spread right across Central and South America and the

Caribbean? She asked herself. All this had been intimated during their poolside meeting with those security people back in Costa Rica, and in the light of all that had followed, she again had absolutely no reason to doubt them, did she?

"You're back much sooner than I'd expected," said Charlie after they exchanged hugs and were sitting together on the living room sofa at Little Oreford Court the following afternoon.

"Yes, I know, but things didn't work out quite as we'd intended," replied Corinne, using the moment to hand back the St Christopher medallion in its little box.

Charlie knew better than to press her daughter for the circumstances, which had indicated that they'd not found out what happened to Brad, so they sat together in a companionable silence for a few moments.

"You know darling, turning up in Little Oreford and finding both you and Laura and that I had two grandchildren and that Robin and Margo were still around, was more luck than any one person has any right to expect in a lifetime," she said quietly

"So I am more than content to leave it at that," she said putting the small box down on the coffee table from where it would be returned to its place in a drawer, destined never to be opened and looked at again.

The Epilogue

Senior Security Officer Alex Gonzales started losing heart in the struggle to uncover corruption in high places in San Jose after Jonathan and Corinne had been so easily snatched from under his nose and nothing had been heard from them since.

It seemed to him that all his attempts to move the investigation forward were blocked by those further up the chain of command, for one reason or another. So he eventually gave up the struggle and requested a transfer back to normal policing duties. His successor, ten years his junior, and both ruthless and highly ambitious, ably assisted by the equally determined Chrissie Morales, eventually got lucky!

Unknown to all those quietly getting on with their lives a world away in Little Oreford, a number of key figures within the Jimarenal Corporation and a clutch of politicians were finally indicted, tried and jailed for periods exceeding twenty years.

Ironically, Brad Junior and his two co directors Antonio and Lucas, were picked up immediately after attending his beloved Papa's funeral in Panama City, where he'd suddenly collapsed and died of a massive heart attack, while staying at the family apartment there.

Corinne's best friend Alicia and her wealthy estate agent husband, Royston, had a baby girl, whom they named Corina.

THE END

NEXT: Read Albany House – Part Four: Affairs In Zurich

Printed in Great Britain
by Amazon